MADE *to* MEASURE MAN

BY

GLEN WEISSENBERGER

ISBN: 0692483489

ISBN 13: 9780692483480

CHAPTER ONE

A TUESDAY IN MARCH

G ARTH MATTHEWS CAREFULLY REMOVED the lid from his Styrofoam coffee cup. He checked to see if the customary warning was embossed on the plastic lid, "Caution Hot Liquid." He thought about the peculiar function of warnings. Frequently, they are designed not to protect the consumer, but rather to insulate the merchant from liability. It is not surprising that Matthews would think about these things. He is a lawyer. When asked what kind of lawyer he was, he would often say, "The worst kind. I am responsible for the creation of two hundred new lawyers a year. I am a law school dean."

This Tuesday morning in March began like a typical day. Matthews had arrived at the office at 8:30 a.m. with his coffee and bagel in a bag. By 9:00 a.m. others who worked in the dean's suite would arrive. That would give Matthews half an hour to eat his bagel and skim several newspapers. At 9:00 a.m., and not before, he would turn on his computer and read his e-mail.

When Matthews was recruited as dean twelve years ago, Chicago Lortigue University had been in existence for five short years. Its board of trustees determined that the newest university in Chicago would grow in prestige if it had a law school. Moreover, the trustees realized that with the proper infusion of resources, the College of Law could be the crown jewel of the University. A highly regarded law school brings virtually any university visibility and academic stature, and there is little room for doubt that Lortigue made the correct decision in forming a law school and providing it with proper funding to excel. It was also clear that Lortigue made the right decision in hiring Garth Matthews as the law school's founding dean.

Lortigue University's history is remarkable as such institutions go. It was founded by the two Lortigue brothers who are heirs to one of the largest European fortunes. The Lortigue family had accumulated wealth since the very beginning of the Twentieth Century, and two world wars and a cold war only strengthened the Lortigue family's control of ever increasing assets. For over a century, the Lortigues rarely put the family name on any of its holdings, not out of modesty, but rather as a means of concealing their wealth from unscrupulous raiders during the wars. The tradition continued into the Twenty-First Century until the two surviving Lortigue brothers decided to use the family name on the founding of Chicago Lortigue University.

Matthews knew the Lortigue brothers well. What had started as a cautious business relationship matured into a genuine friendship, involving visits to the Lortigues' villa in the French Mediterranean village of Neceau. Because of the Lortigues, Matthews enjoyed discrete episodes in his life so lavish that he had no choice but to keep them a secret from every single person he knew. On a day-to-day basis, however, his life was that of a typical law school dean: Faculty meetings, university administration meetings, budget negotiations, fundraising, recruitment of new faculty and American Bar Association committee work. If something really went wrong in his leadership of the law school, the Lortigues could be of no help.

Matthews became particularly close to the Lortigue brothers ten years ago when his wife died unexpectedly of a massive stroke. Jean and Georges came immediately to Chicago and stayed until they convinced Matthews to come to Neceau for an indefinite period of recovery. Matthews' marriage had been strong, and the loss was emotionally devastating.

In Neceau, Matthews regained both his footing and his smile even though the profound sense of loss is not altogether gone even to this day. The Lortigues were perfect hosts and sympathetic listeners. Each had a lost a wife: Jean's wife to cancer and Georges' wife to a scoundrel named Luke DeMarre.

During his stay in Neceau, the Lortigues lavished Matthews with gifts, something they convinced Matthews gave them great pleasure. The Lortigues' Parisian tailor arrived within days and measured Matthews for a wardrobe he never could imaginably afford. The tailor would return on almost a weekly basis bringing jackets, slacks, suits and shirts for meticulous adjustments. The Lortigues' "shoe guy," as they called him, would show up weekly with belts, shoes and leather cases made from the hides of every unprotected species.

Under any other circumstances, Matthews would not have accepted this truly excessive generosity, but more than he liked the new possessions, he enjoyed the obvious delight that Jean and Georges took in planning and presenting the gifts. Consequently, he gave himself over to the process and suspended the boundaries that usually governed his behavior.

Even though Matthews had been given an indefinite leave of absence from Lortigue University after his wife's death, at some point it became obvious to Matthews and the Lortigue brothers that it was time for Matthews to return to Chicago. But the Lortigues consciously made this a careful process as well. The three motored to Paris and spent a few days shopping. Then they flew to London where they went to the theater every night for four days. After that, the three flew to Chicago where the Lortigues kept a watchful eye over Matthews for more than a week.

That was ten years ago.

At 9:00 a.m. Matthews turned on his computer. He usually left the door to his office open, and he could hear his staff's ritual conversations as they arrived. Not that he could discern any complete sentences, but there was a certain rhythm to the banter as they gathered that became more animated as the work week progressed.

Leaving the door open served a number of purposes, certainly one of which was Matthews' desire to be accessible to his staff. It was also something of a necessity because Matthews never bothered to learn how to use the intercom on his phone. Consequently, when he wanted to ask Rose, his assistant, a question, he would raise the volume of his voice and call out her name. For lengthy conversations, he would push his chair with his feet moving backward until he reached the door, a vantage point from which he could converse with Rose face to face.

He looked at his schedule on his computer, and there was one appointment with a person whose name he did not recognize. Propelling his chair backward with his feet, he reached the door.

"Rose, who is this Jeanette Cartere at 11:00 a.m.? Is she from the University?"

"No," was the reply, "She really wouldn't say except that she represented - let me look at my notes - the Schmidhausen Foundation. I tried to get her to tell me if anyone else could help her, but she said, no, she had to speak with you personally."

Rose was superb at keeping Matthews insulated from sales people, complaining students who should really see an associate dean, and misguided people off the street who thought that a law school dean could help them with their legal matters. Consequently, when this Cartere person made it past Rose's screening technique, Matthews was confident that the meeting with Cartere was likely to be of substance.

Rose was more than a secretary and more than an executive assistant, though she definitely functioned in both capacities. Rose was previously the Associate Provost's assistant. When Matthews became the founding dean of the law school, Rose was promoted to her current position, not only because of her superb skills but also because of her remarkable understanding of the inner working of the fledgling university. Matthews would often say that Rose could run the law school on her own, something that proved to be accurate when Matthews took a leave of absence at the time of his wife's death. Over the years Matthews and Rose had developed a bond that was unlike any other in Matthews' life. Rose was his closest confident and his most trustworthy ally. In twelve years there was never a harsh word between them.

Promptly at 11:00 a.m. Rose let Matthews know that Ms. Cartere had arrived. Rose escorted her into Matthews' office, and after the customary offer of coffee or water, Matthews guided Ms. Cartere to the round conference table in his office. As Rose closed the door, she and Matthews shared an almost imperceptible exchange of shrugs, indicating that neither could figure out the purpose of the meeting with Cartere.

Although Rose had not seen Jeanette Cartere before the meeting, if there was a visual component of the screening test, Cartere would have definitely passed it. Cartere was strikingly professional in her appearance. She was neither beautiful nor cute, but her presence definitely commanded attention. Her suit was St. John's knit. Her purse, Chanel. Her nails were a perfect pinkish tan. Her jewelry, which included a wedding ring, was understated. Her engraved business card was simple and dignified, "Jeanette Cartere, Schmidhausen Foundation, Zurich." There was no title or position noted on the card, and the address was simply "Zurich."

"Dean Matthews, you have been dean at Lortigue now for twelve years." Jeanette Cartere spoke with only a trace of an accent which could not readily be identified as German or French. "You have done what is practically impossible. You have taken a law school from its accreditation with the American Bar Association to a position of national, if not international, prominence. In fact, if I recall, the doubters and naysayers whispered that Chicago didn't need another law school. There may have been some truth to what they were saying. Another typical, urban law school may not have been needed. But you have created something that is anything but typical. Lortigue is quite different if not revolutionary. Your curriculum is unlike that of any other law school. Your faculty is exceptional."

"In many ways it's based on a traditional curriculum, but with some..."

"Oh, let's not be silly, Dean Matthews, it's an ingenuous new approach to legal education. And it is your leadership that created it."

"But," said Matthews, "I can't take all the credit..."

"Of course you can, and of course you should," said Cartere interrupting Matthews for the second time. It was clear to Matthews that Cartere wanted to be in control of the conversation, and he politely acquiesced. "Let's not delude ourselves, dean, any team needs the right leadership, and you have provided it. Lortigue's Law School is ranked just after the University of Chicago and Northwestern, and in actuality, it is now a better law school than either of them. Your faculty is comprised of professors who were recruited by you from the best schools, including Harvard, Yale, Chicago and Northwestern but, more notably, your graduates are in greater demand by employers than graduates of any of those schools. The statistics show that your graduates are the highest paid lawyers in the city if they enter law firm practice, and your graduates that pursue public interest work are doing remarkable things, both domestically and internationally. This law school would not be where it is today without your sterling leadership."

Matthews was relieved that his last interjection had not broken Cartere's timing. He was actually beginning to find the monologue quite enjoyable.

Sensing that she would not have to suppress Matthews' modesty again, Cartere continued, "I know you undoubtedly haven't the slightest idea why I am here, and providing that we acted pursuant to our established procedures, that's the way it should be. We operate the Foundation based on definite protocols which we unswervingly follow. Let me tell you that the Schmidhausen Foundation has been carefully watching your career for the last five years."

Matthews started to have a feeling of deflation. This woman, he thought, is going to try to sell him a book with his biography in it. The leather bound version will be two hundred dollars; the cloth bound version, still very nice, will be one hundred dollars.

He was wrong.

"Dean Matthews, every five years our foundation makes a leadership award to one person who has made extraordinary strides in taking an organization or enterprise to great prominence. This year, you have been selected by the Foundation as that person."

Matthews was not sure how to react. He still had a lingering concern that he was being set up to write a check.

"I'm quite flattered," was all he could think to say.

"No, Dean Matthews, make no mistake. This is not flattery." Cartere's tone approached admonishment. "This is an award that involves an extensive investigation and evaluation. The jury takes months to review the dossiers assembled for each potential recipient. And we make only one leadership award every five years. We are not in the business of flattering people. Do you understand that?"

"Yes. Yes I do," replied Matthews as if chastised.

"I know you have many questions, because if we handled this correctly, this award should come as a complete surprise."

"Believe me, it has."

Cartere's delivery was crisp and precise, like a military briefing.

"Well then, let me quickly give you some information. The Schmidhausen Foundation does not make so-called genius awards that give the recipient time off from their positions to work on some project. We think time off is a ridiculous idea. In fact, we only select people who will continue doing precisely what they are doing at the time he or she receives the award. So there will no time off. Is that understood, Dean Matthews? Anyone who can take time off from his or her career is not worthy of the Schmidhausen award. We don't expect the leadership to stop once the recipient is given the award. Is that clear?"

Matthews nodded.

"The award is not widely known because the Schmidhausen family wants it that way. In fact, we will not publicize this award except with a brief press release. You may publicize your receipt of the award but only in ways we authorize. We will make it clear that this is a very prestigious award, but beyond that, the publicity will be limited. Is that understood, Dean Matthews?"

"Yes."

"Your only obligation will be to deliver a few remarks at a dinner in your honor attended by a small group of people. This dinner will be held in New York City because that is where the 86-year-old matriarch of the family, Agnes Schmidhausen, now resides. There was a time when these dinners were held in Zurich, but Mrs. Schmidhausen is too fragile to travel. Let me tell you, however, she is still quite sharp, and she has studied your dossier carefully. In fact, it was Mrs. Schmidhausen who made the final decision on your selection of the award.

"Dean Matthews, I am sure you are wondering whether my credentials are legitimate and that I am disclosing all that is important for now. I suggest you contact Jean or Georges Lortigue. They know the Schmidhausen Foundation, and I have met each of them personally. Our foundation has worked with the Lortigue Foundation on a number of occasions. I can assure you, however, that Jean and Georges had nothing to do with your selection for the award.

"One other thing, Dean Matthews. There is a cash prize that accompanies this leadership award. Over the years, it has become quite large. In fact, no one ever imagined that it would grow to the amount it has and that is why we try not to publicize the award excessively. Most people would not understand. We are pleased to make the cash award in compliance with the terms of the trust. We just don't want the publicity as to the amount to embarrass the recipient, nor do we want the public to infer the value of the Schmidhausen fortune."

Matthews' natural instinct was to blurt out, "How much?" but he exercised restraint and just nodded.

"Of course, Dean Matthews, you would like to know the amount of the award, but you are too polite to ask. All of our recipients, because of their character and sophistication, are too polite to ask. I am certain that in your mind you even asked, 'How much?' I would tell you, but at the moment it is not possible to pinpoint precisely the amount of the award, in part because the award is made without any tax responsibilities for the recipient of the award. What you receive will be all net, free of tax. I can also tell you that the amount of the award will make a difference in your life. The last award, five years ago, was approximately ten million dollars and your award will be at least that much."

"You did say ten million dollars?" The disbelief in Matthews' voice reflected an uncommon understanding of the consequential nature of such an amount of money. As dean, he was an experienced fundraiser who had often explained to a potential donor what could be accomplished with a multimillion dollar gift to the law school's endowment.

"Ten million dollars. It will be deposited in a Swiss bank account." Cartere sounded somewhat impatient.

The meeting ended unceremoniously with only a minimal exchange of words. As Cartere was about to leave the office, she turned to Matthews and managed a thin smile, "Congratulations. You deserve this."

Sitting alone in his office, Matthews mentally replayed the entire meeting with Cartere looking for evidence that he might be the victim of some mean-spirited prank. Could someone be plotting to make him look like a fool? While Matthews believed he had no genuine enemies, he often outwitted those who opposed positions he would take in the governance of the law school. Particularly, his relationship with the University President, Frank Karl, was often fought with tension, but he dismissed the possible complicity of Karl in any scheme surrounding the Schmidhausen award. Karl was too heavy-handed to be involved in anything that required even a small amount of intricacy. Ultimately, Matthews concluded that there was nothing he could do to hasten his understanding of this extraordinary occurrence, and while he was hardly comfortable with simply allowing the facts to unfold, he resigned himself to the reality that he had no other option.

Later in the day, Matthews received the delivery of a leather binder from Jeanette Cartere. Because his day was filled with meetings, during which he did his best not to seem distracted, it was not until he arrived at his home in Lincoln Park after the day's work that he could begin to study the material in the binder.

The binder contained forms for establishing ownership of a Swiss bank account and lengthy descriptions of the terms of the award. He could find no restrictions on the use of the money, and he even found that the delivery of the speech was not a mandatory condition of receipt of the funds. The materials indicated an expectation that the recipient would not donate large portions of the award to charity. As the pertinent language explained, the Schmidhausen Foundation gives generously to numerous causes, and the intent behind the award is to benefit the recipient. Matthews learned that he could discuss the award with the Lortigues, but he could not disclose the amount of the cash award to them when he was apprised of it. There would be no public disclosure of even the existence of a cash award, and consequently, Matthews could not express his gratitude for the cash award publicly. It was, of course, permissible for Matthews to consult an attorney who would handle any legal arrangements regarding the funds.

After reading the material in the binder, Matthews checked the internet for any information he could find about the Schmidhausen Foundation. He found very little. The Foundation's website listed Jeanette Cartere as the only contact person. He e-mailed Jean and Georges to find out what they knew about the Schmidhausen Foundation. He would have tried to call them, but he had no idea where on the globe they were at this moment. He received a prompt e-mail response from Georges who confirmed that the Schmidhausen Foundation was legitimate, and that the Schmidhausen family money originated about the same time as that of the Lortigues.

Georges also added, "They are good people. They have only started reusing the family name about a decade ago." Not certain what Georges meant, Matthews could only assume that the family had been subject to persecution at some point in time during the Twentieth Century. Matthews also knew that when Georges wrote, "They are good people," he undoubtedly meant that their wealth was not derived from corrupt or exploitive activities that were prevalent in Twentieth Century Europe.

At about ten o' clock, Matthews finished reviewing the binder and completing his essentially unproductive internet research on the Schmidhausen Foundation. He went to the library of his house where one of the bars was located and poured himself a few ounces of Macallan 18-Year Old. He often said facetiously that he had several bars in the house because no one should ever be more than fifteen feet away from good Scotch. Hardly a heavy drinker, Matthews did like a good Scotch. His house, a vintage row house in Lincoln Park, was narrow with four living levels. The four bars were really a matter of convenience created by the vertical architecture of the living space.

As he sipped the Macallan, he tried to unwind and grasp the gravity of receiving millions of dollars. Ten million dollars would represent a substantial sum to just about anyone, and while he was financially secure, Matthews could not be described as wealthy. He and his late wife both had law degrees, but neither had been attracted to the lucrative large firm practice. Matthews' wife practiced immigration law and worked at a nonprofit community service organization. Matthews had been a law professor for most his career before being recruited for the deanship at Lortigue.

After reflecting on the matter, Matthews realized that he was totally unprepared to contend with wealth.

CHAPTER TWO

WEDNESDAY

A T 6:45 A.M. WEDNESDAY MORNING, fifteen minutes before his alarm was set to gently rouse him with symphony music, Matthews was abruptly awakened by the telephone. He fumbled to find the phone and said "Hello" into two television remote controls before he finally located the telephone.

"Christine? Oh, this is embarrassing," said Matthews, still in the process of waking up, something that usually required caffeine and several splashes of water to the face.

"Well, you stood me up last night for dinner. I am sure you had a good reason, but you could have called."

Matthews had been casually dating Christine Knowel for about a month. She was blond, very attractive in appearance, and the only person who could possibly fit such a description at the University President's reception for new adjunct faculty where they had met. Christine taught part time in the College of Business and was an attorney in the Chicago office of Manor & Kling.

Still not fully awake, Matthews responded, "Christine, I had what I could only call an unbelievable day yesterday. If you'll forgive me, and if you don't have other plans, let's meet tonight at 7:00 at RL, the restaurant in the Ralph

Lauren building on Michigan. The entrance for the restaurant is on Chicago Avenue."

Matthews was genuinely embarrassed. The lapse was totally uncharacteristic. When he arrived at the office Wednesday morning, even before he pried open the lid on his dangerously hot coffee, he ordered roses to be sent to Christine with a note expressing his sincere apology.

Recognizing that he was inescapably distracted by the Schmidhausen Award, Matthews set low expectations for himself regarding his productivity for the day. Fortunately, there were no major decisions to be made, and scheduled meetings were about largely unimportant matters.

A meeting scheduled for 11:00 a.m. in the morning in the University President's conference room concerned just such an inconsequential matter, despite the fact it was attended by the deans of all the colleges and other high level university administrators.

The meeting was led by Bart Starnover, the Executive Assistant to the University President, Frank Karl. Although in his thirties, Starnover had the stooped posture of a much older man. No one at the University knew his job description, but he was regularly seen carrying food into the president's office. Most often, it was a box of pastries.

Starnover called the meeting to order by saying, "Our purpose here today is to make a recommendation regarding the official portrait of the University President. We have four pencil sketches from which to choose. The President did not wish to influence your choice, and consequently, he will not be attending the meeting."

Four easels lined the front of the room, each covered with a black cloth. Matthews resigned himself to be part of the process, even though his immediate impulse was to get up and leave. Surely everyone in the room had something better to do.

Removing the drape from the first rendering, Starnover explained, "This sketch is a rather standard portrait. As you see, the President is smiling warmly."

Everyone in the room immediately noticed that the picture, even though a sketch, made the President look considerably younger than he was. Moreover, the picture was a sketch of a trim and fit man. President Karl was morbidly obese. Those assembled made barely audible sounds indicating ambivalence at best.

"The second sketch has the President seated. It's essentially the same warm smile. We can add his Persian cat on his lap if you recommend."

The people in attendance variously murmured, "No cat." "No animals," or simply, "Please, no."

"The third sketch shows the President in his academic regalia."

This would be a wise choice thought Matthews because the robe disguised the massive hulk of the President's body. The group's mumblings sounded like approval, but no one could be sure.

"The fourth sketch is very much like the third, but for some reason the President has a mustache. I just received these pencil sketches about an hour ago. It's actually not clear whether the artist put it there or if some prankster added it afterward."

Eric Sythe, the Dean of the School of Nursing, spoke up, "This is obviously sketched from an early photograph of President Karl. He used to have a moustache when he was younger."

"I think the moustache is quite becoming," said Robert Norse, Dean of the Design School.

"I agree," said Matthews. "I think that the President should grow a moustache, and that we recommend portrait number four."

Suddenly, everyone recognized an opportunity to adjourn, and there was a round of applause. All those assembled immediately got up and quickly fled for more important things.

Later in the day, President Frank sent an e-mail to everyone at the meeting thanking them for their advice. He added, "I will indeed grow a moustache," and henceforth, the President's upper lip was adorned with facial hair, at least after a few days' growth.

Matthews spent the remainder of the day trying to deal with matters that required little mental energy. Quite naturally, he could not stop thinking about the Schmidhausen Award. It was a titanic distraction.

Wednesday evening Matthews made it a point to arrive early for his date with Christine. He felt badly that his behavior the previous evening seemed so rude, but he was not exactly sure he could provide Christine with a plausible explanation. He was not at liberty to tell her the truth, and it was not his style to lie. In fact, he was a very bad liar, and he knew it.

Christine made her entrance into the bar at RL right on time. Like most lawyers, male or female, at the end of a demanding day, she appeared slightly fatigued and somewhat tense. Matthews immediately noticed that Christine looked somewhat frayed and agitated, and he was not sure whether she was upset with him or she was merely displaying a lawyer's 7:00 p.m. mid- week countenance.

They found a vacant table in the bar and fumbled over a kiss. Christine went for the mouth; Matthews aimed for the check. They awkwardly connected, but neither hit the target. After they sat down the waiter brought Scotches, both Glenrothes 1991, which Matthews had moments earlier ordered with instructions to serve the drinks when his companion arrived. He selected the Glenrothes because unlike many single malt Scotches, Glenrothes had a sweet, smooth taste. To her credit, Christine was a Scotch drinker, and Matthews thought Christine would like his selection.

Christine shook her head back and ran her hands, open fingered, through both sides of her hair. She immediately appeared more attractive and more feminine.

"I have had the worst day," she began, "Why is it that everything happens at once? I mean nothing really went wrong on these deals, nothing that can't be fixed, but it just all happens at once. Tell me why it is this way. Why does everything become unglued at the same time?"

Matthews smiled with a slight shake of his head. Of course, he wasn't really expected to provide an answer. Christine went on to describe three deals, each of which had encountered a complication that Matthews could only vaguely understand. Matthews was a superb lawyer, but corporate deals were not his specialty. Christine's monologue continued for several minutes and her Glenrothes 1991, which is meant to be sipped slowly, was consumed in healthy swallows. Without breaking stride, Christine gave the waiter the universal hand signal for another round, the index finger pointed downward and moved it in a circular pattern, as she continued to describe one legal calamity after another. Matthews was genuinely entertained by her animation and by her ability to drink strong liquor in a single gulp.

Matthews said very little, except for polite acknowledgments that demonstrated that he was trying his best to follow Christine's story, when the hostess came over to tell them that their table in the restaurant was ready. They picked up their drinks, Christine's new round and Matthews' two rounds, one in each hand, and moved to a perfect, private table in the dining room.

As they settled into their table, moved the tented black napkins to the side, and surveyed the room for people they might know, Matthews realized that he might not have to provide any explanation for his inconsiderate behavior the previous evening. Had he found the perfect woman? Were the roses all that needed to be said? He wasn't sure. He certainly wasn't going to raise the matter if Christine didn't. And she didn't.

Matthews noticed that Christine's face started to look relaxed, and that she was beginning to let go of the frenetic residue of the day. They had only been dating for little more than a month, and Matthews started to feel that she was genuinely interested in him. When women become interested in Matthews, it always felt somewhat surprising to him. This reaction was really a product of his own modesty and not what would be an objective assessment. Matthews was considerably above average in appearance in most ways, but more significantly there was a warmth and kindness about him that most people noticed and liked immediately. As his success in his professional career attested, he was smart and quick to size up a situation. Whenever he was present in a room, it was clear that he was confidently in command. Women beneath his station in life would consider him a good catch, and women above him would consider him an easy project, worthy of the effort.

Referring to the problem with her deals at the office, Matthews offered, "Well, look at it this way: We are in the only business that when something goes wrong, we charge our clients to fix it."

"You're right. And to tell the truth, Garth, I enjoy a good crisis now and then. It keeps everyone on their toes: The client, the secretaries, the associates working with you, and the firm caterer. Don't you miss practicing law?"

"Actually, I do. When I was a law professor in Cincinnati, I had a long term affiliation with a boutique litigation firm. We didn't have any regular clients, but my partner was such a capable litigator that we always had a steady stream of business. We received a lot of referrals from other law firms in the city because our practice was narrowly focused, and we couldn't possibly steal a corporate client. I do miss practicing, but you can't do everything in one lifetime. I truly find being a law school dean to be very rewarding. It's challenging on many levels and requires a variety of skills. I frequently tell people that, figuratively, the deanship requires keeping a massive machine running smoothly, and the machine itself is constructed of dozens of moving parts, each of which has its own energy source. At the same time, a good dean doesn't simply want the machine to run in place, but wants it to move forward on a trajectory that is in alignment with a vision for a better law school."

"Garth, I know you have done wonderful things with the new law school. Everyone in the Chicago legal community is aware of what you have accomplished. Did you anticipate when you were younger that you would be a dean?"

"I am not sure. While I liked the idea of practicing law, I never believed I would make it my entire career. I wasn't certain what I ultimately would end up doing, but one of the reasons I became a law professor was that it seemed like it would lead me to a number of different opportunities. I like new challenges, and I am not afraid to take risks. I certainly have no regrets as to how my career has progressed."

"You are lucky."

"Yes I am. Do you have any regrets?"

"Well Garth, I like the practice, and when things heat up, I really enjoy it. My only regret is that large firm practice can tend to take control of your career and rob you of autonomy. I worked very hard to become a partner, and when I finally made it, I felt it was such an accomplishment that I had no choice but to continue along the same path. Somewhere along this route, however, it felt like others were making career decisions for me. It shouldn't be surprising. A large law firm needs its attorneys to assume specific roles. I'm just not sure that the choices were all my own."

"I understand. Success is never without its costs."

"And a little luck."

"Yes, and a little luck."

Christine was attractive and successful, and she could keep a conversation going. As the conversation progressed, Matthews thought that there might be some potential here. But a sense of potential was all he could feel. Since his wife's death, Matthews had dated several women, but nothing even approximating a strong connection had ever developed. He often hoped that a nascent attraction would flourish into real feelings. It just never did.

CHAPTER THREE

THURSDAY

THURSDAY MORNING AT AROUND ten o'clock, Jeanette Cartere called Matthews on his direct line.

"Can you be in New York tomorrow?" she began. "Mrs. Schmidhausen would like to meet you. While her health is typical of a woman her age, we want to be certain she has an opportunity to meet the person who is receiving the award. You will remember that we make these awards every five years, so you may very well be the last recipient she meets."

A somewhat morbid thought, but Matthews replied cheerfully, "Of course. I can leave tonight."

Matthews wasn't sure what was on his schedule for Friday or the weekend, but he knew that this request, from an eighty six year old woman who was honoring him with such an extraordinary award, was not an invitation that could be declined.

"Dean Matthews, I will have all of the arrangements put in a binder and delivered to you by messenger early this afternoon. I trust you can provide a plausible explanation to your staff as to your sudden absence."

"Of course. That's not a problem."

"And one more thing. We are moving up the award ceremony. It will occur in two weeks from this Saturday. Will that create any difficulties?"

"I am sure I can clear my schedule."

After he hung up, Matthews asked Rose to come into his office and close the door.

"Rose, I need to tell you something in the strictest of confidence."

Matthews knew that Rose would never divulge any information that Matthews had confidentially revealed to her. He was rock certain of her trustworthiness on both a personal and professional level.

"You'll recall that Jeanette Cartere of the Schmidhausen Foundation met with me earlier this week. The purpose of the meeting was to tell me that I am to be the recipient of an award from this foundation. As a general matter, they want to control the information that is released concerning this award. I'm sure they have their reasons, and I certainly want to respect their wishes. At the moment I really don't know all that much about the award, but I am certain I'll learn more because I am going to New York to meet with the matriarch of the family. I need to leave late this afternoon. If anyone asks, just tell them that I am in New York on a personal matter."

"Will you be staying at the Iroquois?" Rose asked.

"Yes, the usual king room or an executive suite."

"By the way, you should be leaving for your meeting at Manor & Kling, and don't forget that you have a meeting with the President at 1:30."

He grabbed his coat and headed for the door for his meeting with Ron Carey, a transactional attorney he used from time to time. A short cab ride took him to the offices of Manor & Kling.

The day previous he had discussed the Schmidhausen Award with Carey by phone. The meeting was probably unnecessary at this juncture, but the Schmidhausen Award was such an unexpected matter, that Matthews felt he should talk to Carey in person sooner rather than later.

When he arrived at Manor & Kling, he was taken immediately to a small conference room with a view of Lake Michigan and Navy Pier. He sipped coffee from a porcelain cup while he waited for Carey.

"Garth, it's been a few years, hasn't it?" said Carey entering the room and extending his hand.

Carey's relationship with Matthews had been limited to legal representation; they did not travel in the same social orbits. Matthews had selected Carey because his firm had frequently represented the University.

"Yes, just about. I think you last helped me with some loose ends regarding my mother's estate in England. This time, however, I think we have something quite different to deal with."

"Yes, it appears we do. I would start out by congratulating you, but getting directly to the point, I have a number of concerns about this matter. I am glad you came to see me before you became too involved."

Matthews did not know what to think or even exactly what questions to ask. He simply stared at Carey indicating that he was ready to listen.

"In performing our due diligence we have undertaken some research on the Schmidhausen Foundation. I had one of our paralegals digging around on this foundation until about 11:30 last night. While their history needs further investigation, I can tell you that they have made deals with questionable people, and their general way of operating is quite secretive."

Matthews experienced a creeping feeling of indignation. He hadn't asked Carey to look into these kinds of matters. But after he absorbed the initial impact of the information, Matthews realized that Carey was only trying to protect him.

"What are you recommending that I do? Decline the award?"

"That would be the safest course of action. It's your decision. At minimum, I think you should keep the Schmidhausen people at arm's length."

"Really?" Matthews mentally questioned how anyone could advise him to walk away from such a large amount of money without further investigation, but then he realized that he had not apprised Carey of the magnitude of the award.

"Yes. For now, you should sit tight. Do not allow yourself to be professionally damaged by any connection with the Schmidhausen family. With your permission I would like to have my paralegal continue to further investigate the Schmidhausens. I might ask someone in our Geneva office to look at this as well. Mainly, we just don't want you to be embarrassed…or worse."

"Or worse?"

"Well, yes."

Carey looked down at the papers in front of him and fidgeted with the paperclip holding them together. After compressing the spring action on the clip a few times, it flew off the paper and hit Matthews in the chest.

"Sorry about that," said Carey recovering the paper clip from the floor. "You see the last recipient of the award five years ago was a Sir Graeme Wooleyfin. He headed a think tank of brilliant economists in London. He built this remarkable operation in seven years. But three weeks after receiving the award, he disappeared. He just vanished into nothingness. The funds in his account were withdrawn, and he just did not show up one day at the office. Of course, one theory is that, contrary to the wishes of the foundation, he just wanted to quit working. He could be in a hammock right now on some island in the Pacific sipping rum from a hollowed out pineapple. The other theory is that, well....."

"Is that he's dead." Matthews finished the sentence.

Carey looked somewhat apologetic. "Yes, well, yes. There are other theories as well, but you have the two extremes."

"Swell."

"So, please have no contact with these people without consulting me. We will investigate this matter thoroughly."

"Of course," said Matthews, but he had no intention of heeding Carey's advice. * * *

Matthews arrived a few minutes early for his meeting with the University President, Frank Karl. Karl was the second University President since Lortigue was founded, and it was almost a universally held opinion that he was far less capable than his predecessor, Andrew McAndrews. From Matthews' perspective, however, Frank's leadership style was tolerable because Frank allowed Matthews great latitude in managing the College of Law. On occasion, however, Frank would try to compel Matthews to do things that reflected the inescapable conclusion that Frank knew nothing about legal education. Matthews was concerned that this meeting would be just such an occasion.

Matthews had often thought that Karl was not a stupid man, but he acted stupidly at critical times. Moreover, he was a terribly bad judge of people. Also not working in his favor was a streak of unmistakable laziness that made him complacent about most things, including the future of the Lortigue University. Always following the path of least resistance and choosing the quick and easy solution, Karl was the embodiment of bad leadership.

Matthews knew that Karl did not put in long days, and spent little time discussing the strategic direction of Lortigue University with his deans and other senior administrators. Karl's idea of a meeting was a protracted lunch where he would eat far more than would be healthy for any living person and talk endlessly with food in his mouth. Frequently, tiny morsels of his lunch would be propelled through his teeth while he was talking, and only the last person who arrived for the meeting would sit directly across from him. His ill-fitting suits were food stained, and he would frequently wear the same suit several consecutive days accumulating additional food remnants as time progressed.

As a complement to his laziness, Karl sought security in his position by maintaining a close relationship with the Finance Committee of the Board of Trustees. The finances of the University were in extraordinarily good order, and Karl never neglected the opportunity to take credit for it. There appeared to be almost an unnatural kinship among the three members of the Finance Committee and Karl. They all were overweight, and all had noticeable food stains on their clothing. Matthews couldn't help but imagine the gluttonous bacchanal that occurred when this group gathered for lunch. He was sure that every conceivable kind of unhealthy food would be on the menu and that food particles would be spewing like a meteor shower.

One of Karl's assistants, Bea White, offered Matthews coffee while he waited, which Matthews gladly accepted. He was on his fourth sip of coffee when Karl opened the door of his office to greet Matthews.

"Garth, it's good to see you. I think it was a brilliant stroke of genius for you to suggest I grow a moustache. Isn't it fascinating the way life imitates art? Come in," said Karl with a grand gesture of his right hand that suited the grandeur of his office.

Matthews had been in the President's office on several occasions, but it never ceased to amaze him how ridiculously garish it was. The room itself was enormous, and the twenty-four foot high ceiling was an architectural odd-ity for a sixteen story building in Chicago's loop. The floor space contained several functional areas, each defined by an oversized exotic carpet. There was a conference table that sat ten; a conversation area that contained several comfortable chairs around a coffee table; a library corner with leather bound books on book shelves with a ladder that slid across a brass rail; an oversized antique writing table which Karl used as his desk; a computer table which ap-peared to be rarely used; and finally, a seating area bounded by three leather couches that occupied the space in front of an enormous masonry fireplace.

"Where should I sit?" asked Matthews.

"Let's sit by the fireplace." Karl's coffee cup was on the table adjoining the couch facing the hearth. An empty box once holding a dozen pastries accompanied the coffee. There was no reading material to be seen in the vicinity of the couch, and it appeared that Karl had been drinking coffee, eating pastries, and staring into the burning fire. From the prevailing odor in the room it seemed that Karl had been belching -- or possibly something a bit more disgusting.

Matthews took his seat on the adjacent couch, and placed his cup and saucer on the table.

"How do you think the moustache is coming along? I think it will take a few days to fill in nicely."

"I think it will make you look very distinguished."

"Garth, there are a couple of things I want you to do." Karl went to his writing table and picked up two files. "Here are files on two applicants I want you to admit to the law school. I know the family in each case. I know these applicants are solid."

Matthews quickly looked through the files, scanning each for critical data.

"Frank, neither of these applicants is qualified for law school. I don't mean to say only that they fail to meet our standards. I don't believe they are quali-fied for any law school."

"That's why their families will be grateful when we admit them to Lortigue."

"Frank, we have had this conversation before. The Law School Admission Test is designed to determine the aptitude of an applicant to be successful in law school. There are times when an applicant has a high grade point average in undergraduate school that compensates for a low LSAT score. But in both of these cases, the GPAs and LSATs are both extremely low."

"How low?"

"The LSAT puts each of them below the 10th percentile. That means that 90% of the test takers performed at a higher level."

"Garth, any idiot can become a lawyer. I want these people admitted. Do you understand?"

"Yes, I understand your position but I am afraid I can't comply," responded Matthews with his customary coolness. "We have a limited number of places in the first year class, and I am obligated to fill them with qualified candidates. The days are gone when law schools admitted marginal applicants and flunked out half the first year class as part of a regime of survival of the fittest. Besides, it will create nothing but bad feelings if these applicants were admitted, and they then flunked out."

"You can see to it that they don't flunk out."

"I am afraid that's not possible," Matthews resisted responding further to the insulting idea that he would manipulate the grades of any student.

"Is there anything else Frank?" said Matthews demonstrating his readiness to leave by standing up.

"Sit down, Garth, there is something else."

"Yes?" said Matthews complying with the President's request.

"The two delegates from the law school faculty to the Faculty Senate are constantly bringing up matters that are potentially embarrassing to me and the Provost."

"Isn't that their job? Isn't the Faculty Senate something of a watch dog entity?"

"Yes, but they are taking their job too seriously. Replace them."

"I can't replace them. They are elected by the faculty as a whole. I have no power to remove them."

"You can find a way to do it," said Karl.

"You can't find what's not there," said Matthews who had now stood up and was heading for the door to act out his disdain with the President's statements.

As Matthews reached the door of the cavernous room, Karl yelled at him without leaving his seat, "I'm tired of your insubordination. I expect my deans to be team players. I need people I can count on. You are a miserable disappointment. And beyond all that, I can't trust a man who is physically fit."

Matthews pulled the door shut as the President continued to yell. Karl's bellowing voice could still be heard after Matthews left the office.

As Matthews exited, he said to Ms. White, "He'll get over it."

"I hear you are responsible for the moustache," said White.

"Yes, I think I am-- at least partially."

"Thanks." The tone of White's statement hardly conveyed gratitude.

As he walked back to his office, Matthews wondered how long it would take for his friction with the President to reach a point of combustion. Surely Matthews' receipt of the Schmidhausen award would make the President feel that he was upstaged, further testing their ability to function within the same University. Were it not for his friendship with the Lortigue brothers, he would certainly feel insecure in his position as Dean.

Matthews decided to disregard his attorney's advice. He would meet with Mrs. Schmidhausen in New York as planned. Matthews was by nature a risk taker, and he enjoyed seeking out new adventures. Compared to other chances he had taken in his life, this one seemed rather small. Ten million dollars, reasoned Matthews, was hardly something any rational person would decline without some investigation. Besides, thought Matthews, what risk could there be in meeting with an eighty-six-year-old woman?

In the cab on the way to O'Hare for his flight to New York to meet Mrs. Schmidhausen, Matthews used his cell phone to call Marlene, Jean Lortigue's personal assistant.

"Yes, Marlene, have him call me on my cell phone at his convenience. I will be in the air with the phone off for a while, so have him leave a message as to where I can reach him. Yes, thanks."

Within minutes, Matthews' cell phone rang. It was Jean Lortigue.

"Jean, I am sorry to bother you, but I am getting some information about the Schmidhausen operation that is concerning me."

"What kinds of concerns are you talking about? Are they asking you to do anything unreasonable?"

"No. No. That's not it. My lawyer at Manor & Kling has been doing some research that raises questions as to some of the dealings of the Schmidhausen Foundation. Despite that, I am headed to New York to meet Mrs. Schmidhausen, and I just want to know if I have any reason to be cautious."

Matthews decided not to even bring up the hollowed-out-pineapple-versus-dead-recipient issue.

"Well, Garth, I am in Miami working on some reef protection matters. How long are you going to be in New York?"

"I had no idea that you were in the states. I would have come down to Miami to see you. In any event, I currently am scheduled to arrive in New York tonight and fly back to Chicago Sunday."

"Where are you staying?"

"The Iroquois. You know next door to the Algonquin."

"Let me check a few things and I'll get back to you. The Schmidhausens always enjoyed an excellent reputation, and in fact, they did heroic things during World War II. I think you are getting bad information about the Schmidhausens, but I will look into it. By the way, I am heading to Chicago this week to attend the reception for the new dean of the Business School. What's his name again?"

"It's Robert Bullock, from Penn."

"Well, I'll see you at the reception. In the meantime I'll check into the Schmidhausens."

"Don't be surprised when you see the President. He is growing a moustache."

"A moustache? Who does he think he is, Teddy Roosevelt?"

"You never really know with this guy."

"You can explain it to me when I see you."

"Thank you so much, Jean. You are a true friend."

"No problem. Call me in the meantime if you run into any trouble."

"Trouble?" questioned Matthews plaintively. "What kind of trouble?"

"Just a figure of speech. You are starting to get a little paranoid. Don't worry. We can deal with this, whatever it is. Take care."

"Take care?"

"Relax. This is not like you."

It was true. It was not like Matthews to get rattled about anything. He was usually balanced and calm in any crisis. In fact, Matthews enjoyed anything that might involve an adventure. What Matthews had learned from Ron Carey gave him some real concern, however, and, of course, the Graeme Wooleyfin matter was more than a little unsettling. His mind started conjuring up bizarre scenarios, further providing a basis for questioning his decision to meet with Mrs. Schmidhausen. Was Wooleyfin a single man? Is the award only given to single men who can conveniently disappear? If there was a nefarious side to what the Schmidhausens sought to achieve by making this award, what could it possibly be? He quickly abandoned these uncharacteristic paranoid ruminations as the cab pulled up to the United terminal.

He went through security and had to wait only a few minutes at the gate before he boarded the plane. Matthews entered the first class cabin and found his seat. Matthews rarely flew first class to New York. The flight was relatively short, and the meal was never worth eating given the fare available at the destination. But Rose had booked the flight earlier that day, and first class was the only available option. He settled into his seat and pulled the New York Times out of his business case.

"You're Dean Matthews, aren't you?" said the thirtyish man in a blue suit and yellow paisley tie who was seated next to him. "I'm Art Nelson. I graduated from Lortigue six years ago. I am extremely proud of the education I received at the law school."

"Nice to meet you. What are you doing now?"

"I am a junior partner at Lavins & Moore."

"Do you know Tim McNarry who is a partner there?"

"Yes. I haven't worked with him, but I hear he is quite a lawyer. We are a pretty large firm, and I only work with a small group of tax attorneys. Excuse me, my phone is vibrating."

Matthews started to have the same uneasy feelings he had when he spoke with Jean Lortigue. He knew every large law firm in Chicago, and there was no firm by the name of Lavins & Moore. And Tim McNarry? That was the name of Matthews' high school basketball coach. Or was it Matthews' high school wrestling coach? It really didn't matter. What mattered was Tim McNarry was not a lawyer, and there was no Lavins & Moore.

The man in the blue suit and yellow paisley tie appeared to be absorbed in paper work for most of the flight. Matthews carefully avoided taking anything out of his business case that had anything to do with the Schmidhausen Foundation or his schedule in New York. He spent most of his time reading newspapers and The New Yorker Magazine. As they left the first class cabin to exit the plane, Matthews and Art Nelson shook hands.

Matthews made his way through the United terminal at LaGuardia doing his best to talk himself out of further paranoid ruminations. Just an ill at ease young lawyer, Matthews told himself. If there was anything deceitful going on, why would he introduce himself? Maybe he was just unemployed and was too embarrassed to admit it. Anyway, how could someone who wanted to look over his shoulder arrange to be seated immediately next to him? The last thought was not that comforting, because Matthews himself once orchestrated being seated next to George Prenopolis, a potential donor to the law school, on a flight from Los Angeles to Chicago. It was no more difficult than having Rose ask Mr. Prenopolis' assistant where he would be seated because Matthews was on the same flight and wanted to introduce himself.

On the cab ride from LaGuardia to the Iroquois hotel, Matthews' cell phone rang.

"Christine? Hi. I am not in Chicago. How are you?"

"I'm fine, but how are you?"

"I'm fine." It was the "but" in her question that signaled more than a salutation. "What's going on?"

"I don't know whether you would approve of this, but I want to tell you that when the 'New Matter' list was circulated yesterday at Manor & Kling, I saw your name. I spoke with the paralegal working with Carey."

Manor & Kling, thought Matthews. Christine is an attorney at Manor & Kling where Matthews' attorney, Ron Carey, is a lawyer. Not a big deal, but why had he not thought of this possible connection? Matthews preferred to keep his legal affairs separate from his personal relationships. Had he given it any thought at all, he would have sought representation by a different law firm.

"Christine, in light of the fact that we are dating, isn't this a breach of ethics or a conflict of interest or at least a violation of firm policy?"

"Oh Garth, I'm sorry, but I was worried about you. I wouldn't have done this if I weren't looking out for your interests. Anyway, there is no ethical violation that I know of. I mean, Carey and I are at the same firm. I certainly wouldn't violate any client confidentiality or anything like that."

"Well, we can debate the subtleties of this some other time. I would just like to keep my personal life separate from my legal representation." Matthews' directness was contrary to his usual diplomatic style, but he was uncharacteristically on edge about the entire Schmidhausen matter.

"Oh my God, you're really upset. Garth, I am incredibly sorry. Maybe my imagination got the best of me. I was trying to do the right thing. Honest. If you were having problems, I wanted to help you. Or if you were in some kind of trouble with the law, I didn't want to get my heart broken."

"Okay, now you are getting just a little bit melodramatic. Of course, I am just a little surprised."

"Well, I really think you should be careful dealing with these Schmidhausen people. They are bad news. Everything I have found about them indicates that you don't want to be connected with them in any way. I am seriously worried about you. Where are you, anyway?"

"I am in Miami. Jean Lortigue asked me to come down to help out with some matters regarding the protection of natural reefs." Matthews knew he was a bad liar, but he thought his deceit might be passable if he was not in a face-to-face situation. His paranoia was running unusually high, and he was unsure of whom he could trust. But mainly, he did not tell Christine that he was in New York because he did not want Ron Carey to find out that he had disregarded his advice to "sit tight."

"Garth, I was hoping we could get together this weekend. When are you coming back?"

"Sunday evening, I think."

"What flight are you on? Can I meet you at O'Hare?"

Now this was the very part of lying that Matthews detested. Lies inevitably become more extended and more convoluted than originally anticipated. The compounding of deceit upon deceit requires a deviousness that was not in Matthews' nature.

"No. I am coming back quite late," said Matthews maintaining a firm grip on his lack of veracity.

"Will you call? Actually, why don't you come to my place for dinner on Monday?"

"Yes, I would like that. We can talk about all of this then."

"How is Miami?"

"It's humid and balmy here, probably around 78 degrees."

This lying stuff is dreadful business he thought.

───

Checking into the Iroquois Hotel gave Matthews a sense of safety. He had regularly stayed there, and it felt like a sanctuary. The hotel itself is small, and despite its Native American name, it feels like a boutique hotel in London or Paris. Most of the staff knew Matthews, and even if they didn't, they were trained to be extraordinarily accommodating to their guests.

"We have the executive suite on five for you, Mr. Matthews. I know you have been in that suite before, perhaps even the last time you were here. It is bright during the day. You will have plenty of room to work in the parlor. We have wireless internet connection throughout the hotel now. There is a bottle of Macallan, on top of the bar, compliments of the manager. We will have the New York Times and the Wall Street Journal for you at the door in the morning."

"Thank you," replied Matthews, "You are always extremely gracious."

The key card was given to John, a bellman who led him up the back elevator to his suite.

Once inside the room, Matthews quickly unpacked and checked the suite's accommodations. Of immediate importance was the ice bucket on the bar filled with fresh ice. There were no ice machines on the guest floors of the Iroquois, and the staff simply checked Matthews' room regularly to make certain that the bucket would be filled with fresh ice. He poured the Macallan over three ice cubes, and waited for the extremely pleasant sound of the crackling of the ice. That subtle resonance had over time created a conditioned response of well-being in Matthews. Thankfully, it had just such an effect this time.

Matthews quickly looked over the schedule that was in the binder delivered to him by Jeanette Cartere. He was to meet Mrs. Schmidhausen tomorrow at noon for lunch at her apartment in the Waldorf Towers at the Waldorf Astoria Hotel. The instructions were to wear a jacket and tie for the private lunch, something he would have done without the prompting.

Matthews sipped the Macallan and was glad to have the evening to himself. He called room service and asked if the chef recommended anything special. He was momentarily put on hold.

"Mr. Garth. This is Chef Stephen. Why don't you come down to the restaurant? We haven't seen you for a while. We have a lovely private table, and we will serve you quickly or slowly, whatever you prefer. I have a lovely wild salmon with a blackberry glaze that I think you would like. I have finally perfected the glaze after several trials."

"Stephen, you are very convincing."

"Can I pair a wine for you?"

"Yes, but by the glass if that's okay."

"Of course."

The dinner was just as promised. The salmon glaze was quite fine. As Matthews was beginning to further unwind, thoughts of the young man with the blue suit and yellow paisley tie faded. He began to have thoughts of Christine, and despite the fact that she had trespassed into his private territory, he did actually like the idea of a woman who cared enough to be worried about him.

When Matthews returned to the room from dinner he noticed that his ice bucket had been refreshed. He also noticed that his business case was latched close. He was almost certain that he had left it open before leaving the suite for dinner. It was something that there was no reason to remember, and he told himself that he was unsure of whether it had actually been left open or shut. When he opened the case and looked through its contents, he found nothing amiss.

Nothing amiss, Matthews thought to himself, in an effort to relax.

CHAPTER FOUR

FRIDAY

F RIDAY MORNING, MATTHEWS AWOKE around 8:00 a.m., 7:00 a.m.
Chicago time. He made an attempt to fall back to sleep because he had
no responsibilities until noon. The effort was futile, however, and he
got out of bed at 8:30 a.m.

He put on a robe and went to the door to pick up his newspapers. He called
room service for coffee and sat down to read the papers. No more than three
minutes later there was a knock at the door.

"Your coffee, Mr. Matthews." Said the man with a tray with a silver pot
and a small vase of flowers. "Can I bring you some breakfast? The usual?"

Matthews nodded.

Coffee, two newspapers, breakfast on the way and more than two hours
of leisure time, thought Matthews, what could be better than that? He spent
the morning enjoying a short respite from the usual frenetic pace of his life.
Rose was masterful at keeping the law school on course when Matthews was
out of the office. She would make a list of matters that needed a decision from
Matthews and would usually go over the list with him by telephone by the end
of the day. A different list contained phone calls he had to return. Rose also
had an uncanny ability to foresee possible crises even if they were distantly
on the horizon.

Shortly before noon Matthews took a cab to the Waldorf Astoria, the entrance of which is on 50th Street, just off Park Avenue. The small lobby, compared with the grand lobby of the Waldorf Astoria, sends a clear message that the suites in the Tower are something very different than the hotel rooms. Matthews carried a small bouquet of flowers and a box of Godiva Chocolates he had purchased before catching the cab.

Matthews asked the woman at the desk for Mrs. Schmidhausen's suite number.

"The fourteenth floor," she replied.

"The number?"

"The fourteenth floor," she repeated.

Matthews nodded and smiled.

He exited the elevator at the fourteenth floor, and he faced an impressive double door, ornate with gilded molding. He rang the doorbell, and the door was promptly opened by Jeanette Cartere, resplendent in her St. John knit. This time, however, her jewelry was noticeably more ostentatious, and she seemed less officious than when they met in Matthew's office. In fact there was something very different about her, but Matthews could not quite pinpoint it.

"Dean Matthews, you are right on time. How lovely to see you again. Mrs. Schmidhausen is looking forward to meeting you."

A maid in a black and white uniform appeared from behind Cartere and took Matthews' coat, and she scurried away quickly as if she had something else important to do.

Matthews was amazed by the grandeur of the entrance hall. The ceilings were at least sixteen feet high, and the hall was extremely wide, apparently in order to accommodate a throng of guests who might arrive at the same moment. Large oil paintings lined the walls of the hall of the type one might expect to see in an English manor house: men in riding gear standing smartly with dogs at their feet; a hunt scene or two; portraits of beautiful women in magnificent flowing gowns; and what was unmistakably a standing portrait of General George Patton, in full military dress.

Cartere led Matthews down the hall until they came to a living room, passing several hallways and doors along the way. The living room was cavernous, and the walls were lined with both huge mirrors and oil paintings. At either end of the living room were large fireplaces, both of which had wood burning fires that filled the room with a mild and pleasant smoky fragrance. Only properly aged hardwood would emit such a pleasing aroma thought Matthews.

Matthews and Cartere stood in the middle of the living room without conversation, as Cartere allowed Matthews to appreciate the opulence of the room.

"This was once General Patton's residence," said Cartere.

Matthews nodded, suggesting that such a fact was not surprising.

They stood quietly for almost a minute until Mrs. Schmidhausen appeared from a door opened by the maid who had taken Matthews' coat.

"Mrs. Schmidhausen, may I present Dean Matthews," said Cartere with an exaggerated gesture of her right land.

Matthews waited to see if Mrs. Schmidhausen would extend her hand. When she did, he shook it gently but firmly, and he gave her the flowers and chocolates.

Mrs. Schmidhausen was a diminutive, kindly looking lady whose appearance seemed quite appropriate for her age. Her hair was white with the slightest blond hue. Unlike some women of great wealth who have had years of plastic surgery that made them look grotesquely deformed, Mrs. Schmidhausen had the natural and healthy face with features that reflected her German lineage. Her makeup was artfully applied, creating a minimalist impression. Her posture was that of a much younger woman, and her hands were small, with skin that was almost translucent.

"Dean Matthews, I mean Garth. May I call you Garth?" asked Mrs. Schmidhausen.

"Of course."

"Well, please call me Agnes, except in public, or course. That would be rude. And you're not rude. I can tell that by your dossier and just by looking at you. In fact, I can tell by looking at you that you are a kind man. You look nice. Very photogenic for the award."

"I am flattered."

"Well don't be. We have had some pretty ugly people who have received the award. That's frequently such a disappointment. Jeanette, remember that Mr. Paris? My god, he was nothing to look at. His teeth were bad, and his nose was, well, big. Remember those huge ears? And his name wasn't Paris; we just called him that because he lived in Paris. Not that I am superficial, I just like good looking people, don't you?"

"Well, I like to consider several qualities."

"You're such a diplomat. I should have expected that. Anyway, you're nice looking."

"Thank you."

Matthews was so surprised by the conversation that he had initially failed to notice that Mrs. Schmidhausen had no accent. He had anticipated a German or Austrian accent, but there was no trace whatsoever.

"Well, Garth, let's sit down and have something to drink before lunch."

Matthews smiled politely.

The maid appeared, or perhaps she had never left. The room was vast, and the conversation had kept Matthews' eyes riveted on Mrs. Schmidhausen.

"What shall it be Madam?" said the maid.

"Today I will have an extra dry Gin Martini with olives and onions. And put it in an Old Fashioned glass. Those Martini glasses are easy to spill. And Jeanette?"

"Oh, I think I'll have a Bloody Mary, heavy on the vodka."

"Dean Garth, what about you?" said Mrs. Schmidhausen.

"I usually don't drink during the day…"

"You do drink, don't you?" said Mrs. Schmidhausen.

"Well, yes, I do…"

"And you don't have business to conduct this afternoon, do you?"

"No. Actually, no I don't."

"Then don't be so stiff. Loosen up. You're here to celebrate. You must have a drink. You drink Scotch don't you?"

"Yes I do, but today I'll have the same as Mrs. Schmidhausen," said Matthews nodding to the maid. "Yes. In the same kind of glass. I agree those martini glasses are nothing but trouble."

"Hers will be a double. Would you like yours to be a double as well?" asked the maid.

"No. A single will be fine."

"Dean Garth, I must say, you are a fine person," began Mrs. Schmidhausen. "Your dossier was very strong. It is never easy to make our selection, but this time you were considerably ahead of the other candidates. It's so damn hard to find leaders these days. Those politicians in Washington are the worst of the lot. You see, we are not looking for someone who did something heroic, and we are not looking for someone who made an amazing discovery. And we are not in the business of giving lifetime achievement awards. Rather, we look for someone who shows remarkable leadership in taking an organization or entity from nothing to something really extraordinary, something that makes a genuine impact on society. You see, my grandfather was just such a person. He amassed a fortune in just eight years. He manufactured soap with unique fragrances. Previously in central Europe, soap really smelled like tar. People were clean after bathing with this soap, but they smelled worse than they did before the bath. He developed perfumed soap based on the simple belief that people didn't want to smell like tar after they bathed. We use his life as standard for the award. If we smell tar in the candidate's dossier, he doesn't have a chance."

Matthews realized that despite her eccentricities, Mrs. Schmidhausen still had her mind, and it was sharp. As to Grandfather Schmidhausen, Matthews was impressed. Who would even bother to bathe if the result would be smelling like tar? Anything that encouraged more bathing was laudable, thought Matthews.

"Ah! The drinks are here. Let's get down to business. I would like to propose a toast to Dean Garth, a talented leader, a shining intellect, a man of integrity, someone who knows how to celebrate when the time is right and a really nice looking guy. And frankly, Grandfather Schmidhausen would approve of you, because you actually smell rather nice."

Matthews was repeatedly surprised by Mrs. Schmidhausens' behavior, but not as much as by what happened next. Mrs. Schmidhausen took her gin filled Old Fashioned glass in her hand and drank it completely without having it part from her lips. He looked over at Cartere, and she did the same, leaving tomato juice on her upper lip. No choice thought Matthews: He drank down his gin in the same manner. He waited to see if either of them threw their glasses into the fireplace, but it did not happen.

"Another round, Gracie," called Mrs. Schmidhausen to the maid, and the maid took up the glasses on a silver tray and reemerged so quickly that it was evident that some unseen member of the staff had already prepared the second round.

Mrs. Schmidhausen sipped the second Martini, giving Matthews a sense of relief that he could permissibly do the same. He looked over at Cartere, however, who was drinking her second Bloody Mary rather quickly. It was not a one gulp maneuver, but she was drinking it as if it contained no vodka. Cartere started to appear somewhat odd in a happy sort of way. Her posture had changed. Her right shoulder had slumped, and her head was bobbing ever so slightly.

Matthews and Mrs. Schmidhausen spent the next fifteen minutes or so talking about Lortigue University College of Law, and she asked several questions that reflected a remarkable understanding of legal education. She questioned Matthews about the graduates' bar passage rate, their placement in legal positions and the U.S. News and World Report ranking of law schools. She inquired about the faculty's published scholarship. Despite feeling an effect from the liquor, Matthews answered the questions coherently. Meanwhile, Cartere asked for another drink, which became a third round for everyone. Matthews discretely placed his drink on a table and left it there untouched. As they moved into the dining room for lunch, it was clear that Cartere was completely inebriated. Matthews was struggling to act like he was sober. And Mrs. Schmidhausen appeared unaffected.

As they took their seats around the table in the dining room, Cartere began the conversation.

"Dean Garth, I agree with Mrs. Agnes that you are a most deserving candidate. You are really a good leader, a fine person, a good man, a real gentleman and I agree that you have a nice smell…"

"Jeanette," said Mrs. Schmidhausen sternly. "Enough!"

"Yes, Mrs. Agnes," said Cartere as she muffled a small belch with her napkin. "I was just trying to participate in the conversation."

"Well," said Matthews, "I think you are both charming ladies, and I am having a marvelous time." It was the only thing he could think to say. And it was truthful. Their eccentricities were benignly amusing. Clearly, nothing calamitous could result from meeting with them.

"Well that is what we want. We like to have fun," said Mrs. Schmidhausen, "The rest of the award stuff is, well, stuffy."

Matthews chuckled dutifully.

"I just wanted to have time to get to know you as a person," said Mrs. Schmidhausen, "Ah, the lunch is coming in. It's sliced Kobe beef salad. The tomatoes are grown in a hot house on the roof of this building, so even in the winter they are worth eating. Bon appetit." Three servers placed domed plates before each person seated at the table. On some silent cue, they lifted the domes simultaneously.

The wine was served, a red varietal that had been decanted and, consequently, Matthews really didn't know its provenance. Probably French, he thought.

The conversation continued to center around the law school. Then Mrs. Schmidhausen abruptly changed the subject.

"Now, Dean Garth," said Mrs. Schmidhausen, "there is a moral component of this award."

Cartere seemed to perk up.

"Moral component?" questioned Matthews, sipping the wine which, while he could not identify it, he thought it was very fine.

"Yes. You see, we know you haven't robbed any banks or have been disbarred in any state. No felonies. No drunken driving. No history of drug use. But…"

The two women looked at each other, and Cartere suppressed a giggle.

"But… frankly, you have been a single man for several years."

Cartere had finished her first glass of wine, and a male member of the staff materialized and poured her a second glass. She kept trying to suppress a giggle. Her right shoulder was slumping further, and it appeared she was at risk of falling off the chair. She didn't fall, but she was listing heavily to starboard.

"Dean Garth, your personal life is hard for us to research. You know, we talk with people, but folks just aren't forthcoming about those things."

At this point Cartere started to outwardly giggle. She was not holding her liquor well at all, and she was becoming giddy just anticipating the remainder of the conversation.

"Oh, don't mind her," said Mrs. Schmidhausen. "She probably had a few before you came… Well, Dean Garth, we just don't want a situation here like we see with so many politicians and sports figures. You know, someone coming out of the bushes after we announce the award claiming that you are the father of her child."

Cartere was in full bore laughter, although her head was buried in her napkin. Mrs. Schmidhausen ignored her as if she had tolerated this behavior in Cartere regularly.

"Well, Mrs. Agnes, I have been a single man for several years…"

"So you have illegitimate children?"

"No. No, I don't. But I haven't been, well, celibate since my wife died." Matthews tried to sound unapologetic.

"So, you have been spreading your seed far and wide?"

Cartere was beside herself. She hadn't laughed so hard since the last time Mrs. Schmidhausen had a similar conversation with a Frenchman nominated for the award. Her napkin continued to muffle her laughter and her occasional belches.

"Far and wide? No, I don't think so. I have had very few serious relationships since my wife died, and none of them…."

"Bore fruit," interjected Mrs. Schmidhausen.

"Bore fruit!" exclaimed Cartere. "That's the term the Frenchman used. Oh my God, this is good…"

Mrs. Schmidhausen looked disapprovingly at Cartere. But Matthews thought that this was more an orchestrated charade than actual disapproval. She obviously put up with this behavior in Cartere and, thought Matthews, probably found it more entertaining than embarrassing. Moreover, Mrs. Schmidhausen was doing her share of drinking, and Cartere was an excellent foil who made Mrs. Schmidhausen appear quite sober.

"No, there's been no fruit," answered Matthews.

"Well, good. Just keep your tallywacker in your pants. It's only two weeks until the award."

"I can keep my, ah, tallywacker in my pants for two weeks, I assure you."

"Good. One more thing now that we have the tallywacker matter tucked away, I have a favor to ask of you. My granddaughter would like to meet you. She is a professor at Hunter College. She was on the Schmidhausen jury that selected you. As someone in academia, she has a special appreciation and admiration of your leadership."

"Of course. I would be pleased to meet her." What else could he say?

"Then she will call you on your cell phone. We have the number."

"When?"

"She would like to meet you tomorrow if you are still in the city."

"Yes. Yes, of course."

Matthews left the Waldorf and took a cab back to the Iroquois.

Upon returning to his suite at the Iroquois, Matthews immediately went into the bathroom and soaked a washcloth in cold water. As he leaned back to let gravity hold the wet cloth on his face, the water trickled down his neck and into the collar of his shirt. He felt slightly ill. He truly disliked drinking alcohol during the day. A beer with lunch was not a problem, but this had been gin and wine.

After drying his face with a towel, he removed his jacket and tie and climbed into bed. He stared at the ceiling and tried to make sense of the lunch with Mrs. Schmidhausen and Cartere. It was certainly a strange lunch, much like a party conceived by Lewis Carroll, but nothing about it would suggest that there was anything nefarious behind the award. If anything, Agnes and Jeannette seemed too eccentric to concoct anything truly evil. As he replayed the entire episode in his mind, he started to smile. The smile became broader, and he started to laugh when he thought about his commitment to keep his pants zipped. Thinking about Agnes Schmidhausen and Jeanette Cartere, he recalled what Lewis Carroll's Alice said to the Hatter, "You're entirely bonkers. But I'll tell you a secret. The best people are."

His stomach felt more settled, and he lapsed into a deep sleep.

At around 4:30 in the afternoon, Matthews was awakened by the ring of the phone. A bit disoriented, he picked up the hotel phone and heard a dial tone. The phone continued to ring, and he realized that it was his cell phone in his jacket which he had tossed on the chair. He reached into two pockets before finding the phone.

He answered the phone with his customary greeting, "This is Matthews."

"This is Christine," she said playfully mocking his words. "I am just checking up on you. Is everything all right?"

"Yes. Yes, of course." Matthews quickly tried to shake off his slumber to remember where he told Christine he was. He knew he had lied about New York, but for a moment he could not remember his fictional location. One of the dreadful aspects of lying is that it involves a keen memory for fictitious facts.

"Everything is fine. In fact I was just taking a nap," he said, to buy a little time.

"Garth, I just want you to know that I am concerned about you. I have been doing some more research on the Schmidhausens. Their family may have been involved in some really nasty business. I will explain it to you when you get back."

"What kind of nasty business?"

"Well, that's not clear, but I've done some research on my own. Let's just say that it appears to be narcotics and possibly trafficking in the sex trade. During most of the Twentieth Century their dealings were above board, but recently they have been using their money in questionable ways. I really think you should just decline the award."

"Where are you getting this information?"

"Garth, I really can't say, but I really want you to keep them at arm's length. Don't meet with them. Don't speak with them on the phone. These are not the sort of people you can trust. They could really put you into situations that would be totally embarrassing if not professionally damaging."

"I certainly wish you could be more specific."

"I can't at the moment. You will just have to trust me. Well, how is Miami?"

"Miami? Oh, it's pleasantly warm." The lying made him feel most uncomfortable. "I hear Jean at the door. I have to go."

"Be safe."

"I will."

Matthews was genuinely troubled by Christine's admonitions regarding the Schmidhausen family. But it was all so vague. There was nothing concrete that his lawyer, Carey, or Christine were telling him. It did feel awful, though, that he had lied to Christine concerning his whereabouts.

His guilty ruminations were interrupted by the ring of his cell phone.

"This is Matthews."

"Dean Matthews, this is Julia, Agnes Schmidhausen's granddaughter."

"Yes. She mentioned that you would call."

"Well, I must say that my grandmother is quite impressed by you. She even told me you smelled nice."

"That's good to hear. I found her to be quite charming. She was full of surprises." Matthews quickly wondered whether that was the right thing to say.

"That she is. She never fails to surprise me, that's for sure."

Matthews was relieved by her response.

"Garth--May I call you Garth?"

"Of course."

"Garth would you meet me for lunch tomorrow?"

"Will you be joined by Mrs. Cartere?" Matthews had to ask. He would not have declined the invitation, but he wanted to know whether he should prepare himself.

"Oh my God, no" replied Julia with a laugh. "I don't know why my grandmother puts up with that woman. But then, sometimes I don't know why Jeanette puts up with my grandmother. You would think they would drive each other to the madhouse, but in fact they seem to accomplish remarkable things. It must be some kind of bizarre symbiosis."

She laughed again. Matthews immediately liked her laugh.

"Garth, there is this lovely French restaurant on 71st, just off Madison Avenue. It's the Le Cheval Blanc. Can you meet me there at noon?"

"Yes, of course. How will I know who you are? Do you resemble your grandmother?"

"Not at all."

Matthews was relieved by the emphatic nature of her response.

"It's a small restaurant. They know me. I'll get there a few minutes early and be seated. You can just ask for my table."

"I'll be there at noon."

Matthews liked Julia's laugh, but he wondered whether it could be a mistake to agree to meet with her. Having lunch with Julia would certainly not heed Christine's admonition of keeping his distance from the Schmidhausen family, and Christine would be truly upset with him if she knew he planned to have lunch with Julia. But Matthews had become fascinated by the Schmidhausens, and he did not want to offend a family that selected him for the extraordinary award that bore the family name. Equally important, he was on an adventure, something he always found to be an enjoyable diversion from the demands of his everyday life. None of his previous adventures, all of which seemed more risky, had created any disruption in his life, and he could not imagine that meeting Julia could potentiate any real danger.

Friday evening Matthews ordered room service for dinner and watched Hitchcock's "To Catch A Thief" on the classic movie channel. He fell asleep watching the second feature, Hitchcock's "North by Northwest," a film he had seen several times.

CHAPTER FIVE

SATURDAY

A S MATTHEWS RODE IN the cab to meet Julia, he wondered if she would be as odd as her grandmother. He recalled the novels of Edith Wharton which he read in his high school literature class. A frequent theme in Wharton's novels is that wealth, real wealth, has a way of making people quite different from the remainder of society. His mind then jumped to the question of whether the Schmidhausen monetary award would be sufficient to change his own personality. He was not sure of the amount of the award, but it appeared that it would be substantial, and this potential status as a person of wealth had not as yet prompted much reflection. Of course, he would continue as dean of the law school. His day-to-day lifestyle would not change because he would not want the people who surrounded him to have an inkling that his financial position had radically improved. Matthews then thought about his vacations: They would certainly change. With only the scrutiny of strangers, he could live as lavishly as he pleased. Many of his peers traveled to foreign countries, and travel in itself would not arouse suspicion. And if he stayed in the largest suite in the London Savoy Hotel, no one in Chicago would have to know.

As the cab continued to head north on Park Avenue, Matthews felt a mild but pleasant sense of exhilaration from the prospect of meeting Julia.

He genuinely enjoyed meeting her grandmother, and this adventure seemed to present even fewer risks. Matthews had begun to discount his lawyers' advice completely. Until Christine or Ron Carey provided him with concrete reasons to avoid the Schmidhausen family, he decided to proceed on the premise that he would gladly accept the rather extraordinary monetary prize. He rationalized that he could withdraw from the process at any time before actually accepting the award.

For some reason, Matthews started to think about how he might use the money from the Schmidhausen award. He was not the type to indulge in extravagance, but the remarkable amount of money tended to redefine what might be considered an indulgence. He decided that when he returned to Chicago, he would start looking for a vintage, two seat, Jaguar convertible, something from the late forties or early fifties. This wasn't the first time he thought about a Jaguar. Matthews often wondered why he had always wanted such a vehicle. He couldn't use it for a trip. He wouldn't dare park it on the street and leave it unattended. Its only real function, other than using it for the pure enjoyment of driving such a remarkable vehicle, would be to drive it to a friend's house where it could be parked off the street. Practically without function, thought Matthews, but that's why it's called an indulgence. If he accepted the Schmidhausen Award, it truly would be a very small extravagance.

The cab let Matthews off at Le Cheval Blanc which was adorned by a sidewalk placard with a white horse smoking a cigarette. Le Cheval Blanc was typical of many small Manhattan restaurants: Its only natural light was from the windows bordering the street. Long and narrow, the most private tables were toward the back. Noon was somewhat early for New York Saturday lunch, but a number of the tables were already filled.

"Has Julia Schmidhausen arrived?" asked Matthews to the hostess.

"Miss Julia? Yes, she has. Would you like to be seated, or do you know her table?"

"I would like to be seated."

The hostess led Matthews to the back of the room where the lighting was dim, and where the candles on the table served a genuine function. Matthews was taken by complete surprise when he saw Julia who was seated with her back to a wall. He had expected to see a stereotypical Manhattan social-ite with accoutrements similar to that of Jeanette Cartere. Julia, in startling contrast, was wearing jeans and a severely faded Hunter College sweatshirt that was once, most probably, a shade of crimson. Her tortoise shell glasses tended to slip down her nose, and her hair was either black or dark brown. She looked young, very young, actually. Young enough to be a student rather than a professor, thought Matthews, and a freshman at that. Her face was sweet but rather plain in the dim light, perhaps because it was lacking make up of any kind.

"Dean Matthews," said Julia extending her hand, "It is really nice of you to make time to meet with me. Please sit down."

"Yes. Thank you," said Matthews taking his seat. Matthews noted in his mind that Julia lived up to her statement: She did not resemble her grand-mother. Not in the least. He hoped the lack of resemblance was not limited to her physical appearance, but her drinking habits as well. He scanned the table and was relieved to see that Julia had a glass of ice tea in front of her. There was no liquor in sight.

"You teach at Hunter? That's right around here, isn't it?"

"Yes. We're practically on the campus. I think the college owns this prop-erty and most of the block, probably."

"Some students at the law school have been graduates of Hunter. I think they were mainly political science majors. Great students; they all did quite well. What do you teach?"

"I teach art history. Most of my students do not go on to law school. In fact, I can't think of one that did. The successful ones go on to get advanced degrees. It is a fascinating subject, but there aren't many jobs for art history majors."

Matthews quickly concluded that Julia had to be extremely intelligent, not because of anything she said, but rather because of the objective fact that aca-demic positions in the humanities are awarded to a very select group of can-didates who have PhD's from only a handful of elite universities. The thought crossed Matthews's mind that perhaps Julia's grandmother had exaggerated in describing her as a "professor." She might be a teaching assistant or a graduate fellow, thought Matthews.

"How long have you been at Hunter?" asked Matthews. The answer might reveal what type of position she had.

"I started at Hunter right after I completed my doctorate. It has been my only appointment. Let's see, I've been at Hunter twelve, almost thirteen, years."

Matthews quickly did the calculation in his head. He was astounded by the result. If his math was correct, Julia was much older than she appeared. Unless she was one of those extraordinary geniuses who graduated from college when she was fifteen, her age would be approaching forty.

Now Matthews was curious. He was about to ask her a question which might reveal her age when the waitress came to the table.

"Please order, Julia. I'll be ready in a matter of seconds." Matthews was adept at quickly reading a menu, and after Julia ordered the duck a l'orange, Matthews ordered the Dover sole to be preceded by a small field green salad with strawberries and red raspberries.

"What period of art history is your specialty?"

"In my teaching I am something of a generalist because I don't have the seniority to teach only graduate students. My published writing, however, is on Old Master landscapes. Most people are fascinated by the portraits, but the landscapes were almost never commissioned, and consequently, they reflect work that the artist actually wanted to paint, or work on which he honed his skills. I also have studied still life from this period, but they tend not to be the artist's strongest work."

"Old Masters? What time period are we talking about?" Matthews was really quite cultured, but he wanted to ask an expert the question.

"Well, most people define an 'Old Master' as a work that was painted by a skilled European artist who worked before 1800. The starting date of the period is during the Thirteenth or Fourteenth Century, depending on the authority. Of course, it is hard to pinpoint these dates with any real precision. For example, in pragmatic matters, Christie's defines the period as ranging from the Fourteenth to the early Nineteenth Century. This definition would, for example, include Delacroix who died in the 1860's."

Matthews studied her as she unguardedly spoke about a subject on which she was a confident expert. He watched the expressive use of her hands and studied her face which had a warm quality that would not be expected from someone discussing art history. He also noticed her posture, which had the quality of confidence and carriage that was that of a person beyond her twenties.

"I also have written papers on the 'degenerate art' as a counterpoint to my work on the Grand Masters."

"Degenerate art?"

"Exactly. My work is on the pieces of degenerate art that were destroyed after 1937 in Nazi Germany. Many of these works are identifiable only through secondary images, such as photographs."

"What falls into this category?"

"Well, there is nothing degenerate about it. It was only called 'degenerate art' in Nazi Germany, but Germany dominated the preservation and destruction of art in Europe during the period between the mid 1930's until the mid-1940's. It is essentially contemporary art that Hitler thought was contaminated by Jewish cultural influences and other 'degenerate' influences. It includes works by Klee, Chagall, Matisse, Miro, Picasso and many others. Of course, Hitler was wrong about this art as he was about most things. Many of the pieces from this period were recovered by the former Society Union and are on display in the Hermitage Museum in Saint Petersburg. Most of it, however, was simply burned by the Nazis. It was really quite tragic."

Matthews sat quietly for a moment having learned something about a subject he previously knew very little, a rare occurrence in a short casual conversation. He also continued to observe Julia who was starting to look more mature because of her manner of speech, her subtle body movements and her incredibly expressive face. In fact, he began to find her attractive.

Matthews was served his salad which he offered to share with Julia. She accepted the invitation and used her bread plate as a receptacle for half of the field greens. He recalled his earlier puzzlement about her age.

"Julia, tell me a little about your career. Are you being considered for tenure soon?"

"Actually, I am tenured. I was promoted to full professor about three years ago."

Matthews was genuinely impressed. The choices were clear: She was either a prodigy or she was older than he had originally gauged.

"So you must be one of those extraordinary geniuses who graduated from college in your mid-teens."

"No. I graduated from college when I was twenty-two. I did have the resources to work on my doctorate at a steady pace, but I set no speed records for my academic studies. Really, I traveled a great deal during that period of my life. The art that I studied for the most part is not in the United States, and I spent a great deal of time at the art centers around the world."

Without a segue, Matthews said, "Well, you are correct. You don't resemble grandmother."

"No I don't" replied Julia, without being entirely certain that Matthews was making a statement about her appearance. "The reason we look so different is that my mother was Vietnamese. She was a member of the Nghiem family...."

"Yes, I know of the Nghiem family name. If I recall correctly, they historically had a close alliance to the French and other Europeans."

"Yes. My mother was living in France when she met my father."

"'Julia,' that's not your Viet Nam name, is it?"

"I never had a Viet Nam name, but my father who was fluent in Vietnamese used to call me 'Bion'."

"Bion? What does that mean in English?"

"It is an obscure name, but it roughly translates to 'secretive' or 'mysterious.' I actually think that the closest English word is 'enigmatic'."

"Enigmatic: Does that apply to you?" Matthews smiled warmly to indicate that he really wasn't prying into her personality.

"Well, my father thought so. My mother would call me 'Linh' which means 'gentle spirit' or 'gentle soul' or something like that. I suspect I am such a complex person that either name could apply. It has been a long time since anyone has used the names. But I have confided in you, and now you can use any of the three names, depending on how you feel about me at the moment: Julia, Bion or Linh."

"Well, frankly, at the moment I would think of you as Bion, because you appear to be so young, even though so accomplished."

"I know, the youthful appearance is a family trait, at least on my mother's side." Julia shook her hair into her face and pulled her hands into the sleeves of her sweatshirt, mimicking the way her female students often presented themselves in her office. She was immediately transformed into a younger person.

"How old do I look now?" she said playfully.

"Eighteen."

"Damn. I am getting old. The last time I tried this, the person guessed sixteen. Garth," she said, with a mischievous sweet smile as if making a secret confession, "I am thirty nine, almost forty."

"I am astonished," said Matthews. "I really am."

Julia blushed slightly – but perceptibly.

"I guess I should tell you some things about me," said Matthews changing the subject, thinking that he had possibly embarrassed Julia.

"I would love to hear it. But I should warn you. I carefully studied the dossier prepared for your candidacy for the Schmidhausen Award. I probably know more about you than you could ever imagine. For example, I even know what your grades were in college."

The waitress approached the table with their entrées and filled their water glasses. Matthews and Julia talked about Matthews' career, but he found that Julia really did know a remarkable amount of information about him, including some things he had himself forgotten. Julia recited data about Matthews' college organizations, his Law School Admission Test score, his friends, his past friends, his preferences in food, wine and liquor, the real estate taxes he paid on every residence he had owned, his tailor, his childhood pets' names, where he bought his bagel and coffee in the morning and several other rather obscure facts about him. Matthews was amazed, and simultaneously amused by Julia's ability to recall such detailed information. They also talked about the faculty politics at their respective colleges, and laughed about the ridiculous behavior of some of their colleagues. An eavesdropping, objective observer would conclude that Matthews and Julia were having a fine time, and that would be quite accurate.

It was 2:30 when they finished their hot tea. Matthews found it hard to believe that the time had passed so quickly.

As they were leaving Le Cheval Blanc Matthews realized that he had not discovered whether Julia was single. He found himself wanting to know. Compared to her knowledge of his life, his knowledge of hers was quite meager. Julia, however, put this issue to rest when she surprised Matthews with an invitation.

"Garth, I have been invited to a party tonight at the home of Henry Posse. He came to one of my public lectures. After the lecture, he spoke with me, and he boasted that he had a collection of Old Masters in his place on the Upper East Side. Actually, he claims that he has an even larger collection in his house in Huntington, on Long Island. I found him a little strange, even creepy, but I accepted the invitation because I am eager to see his collection. I think this will be a fairly large party, so we can blend in and leave early once I have seen the collection. I would really appreciate it if you would join me as my date."

Matthews was eager to accept the invitation not only because he found Julia to be intriguing, but he also suddenly found himself feeling protective of her. In complete disregard of Christine's advice to keep his distance from the Schmidhausen family, and without hesitation, Matthews replied, "Of course, I would love to go with you."

"Oh, thank you. I am very grateful. I will pick you up at the Iroquois at 8:00. I really don't know what other men will be wearing. If it's an artsy crowd, the style could be anything from the Village People to tuxedos. If it's a normal crowd, I think they may be more formal than the sweater and jeans set. If you have a sport coat, or better yet, a navy blazer, that would be a safe bet."

"Are you sure that I will fit in?" asked Matthews.

"For God sakes, Garth, you are a law school dean and an extraordinary one at that. You're so presentable, I could take you anywhere."

After leaving Le Cheval Blanc, Matthews and Julia walked in opposite directions on Madison Avenue. Matthews headed south knowing that the

Ralph Lauren store was a few blocks in that direction. He did not have a navy blazer with him on the trip, and he decided that he would simply buy one, despite the fact that he already had two blue blazers at home. Julia suggested a navy blazer, and that's what he would wear.

As he walked south on Madison, Matthews marveled at the amount of information about his life that Julia not only knew but had committed to memory. Had these facts been collected for any purpose other than for his consideration for a rather prestigious award, Matthews would have found this exercise intrusive. But, thought Matthews, if someone is going to give you millions of dollars for a leadership award, that benefactor better know everything possible about you. Nevertheless, Matthews was certain that if he reported this incident to Christine, she would be convinced that it was all part of a sinister plot. Equally, Ron Carey would be offended that Matthews had not heeded his advice.

Matthews momentarily wondered whether the award was just a pretext to gather extensive, detailed information about him. But, he thought, even an amateur can find a vast amount of information about everyone just by searching the internet. He quickly dismissed the pretext theory.

Matthews had shopped at the Ralph Lauren store on Madison before. He was a frequent customer at the Chicago store on Michigan Avenue, and he had also shopped at the Ralph Lauren store on Rodeo Drive in Beverly Hills. The stores had extensive inventories, much more than what would be found in department stores carrying the Ralph Lauren label. As a general matter, Matthews liked the Ralph Lauren look, which he jokingly called neo-classical.

Once inside he found himself for the first time thinking like a person who had limitless resources. The price of an accessory or an item of clothing became largely irrelevant. If he liked it, he bought it.

Before leaving the store he had selected several ties, a half dozen shirts, cuff links, and a Purple Label suit, all to be sent to his residence in Chicago. As to the navy blazer, he found one with bone buttons that seemed at least somewhat different than the ones he already owned. The sales associate was most accommodating in assuring Matthews that the alterations on the blazer could be done that afternoon and that the jacket would be delivered to the Iroquois by 5:00 p.m.

None of the purchases were truly extravagant, and he would put all of these acquisitions to good use. Nevertheless, the experience of purchasing clothing without a conscious consideration of price was intoxicating, and Matthews realized that such extravagance in buying cars, yachts and other purchases much costlier than apparel could lead to disastrous consequences. For the first time, Matthews began to truly appreciate how people with new financial wealth could find themselves destitute in a relatively short period of time. He left the store and emerged into the bright sun and fresh air. He breathed deeply to clear his head.

It was a pleasantly sunny day for March, and Matthews decided to walk back to the Iroquois and window shop at the stores along Madison Avenue. As he passed clothing shops with European names, he realized that Ralph Lauren was hardly the priciest label available. He walked past stores with windows displaying men's watches, many of which did more than merely tell the time of day. Matthews owned a few watches, but not one of them cost more than $2,000. For some people a $2,000 watch would seem ridiculously expensive, but for a person with resources and a taste for exquisite watches, $500,000 would not be an excessive price. Matthews thought that one day he might buy an expensive watch, but not today. The intoxication of the Ralph Lauren shopping experience had worn off, and Matthews felt grateful that it had.

Once back in his suite at the Iroquois, Matthews checked his e-mail and phone messages. While he had his computer on, he decided to check the Hunter College website to find out more about Julia. He was curious about her education. When he found the Hunter website, he used the search function to look for Julia but discovered that the search led to a screen that stated: "Search results for Julia Schmidhausen: Not found."

Not found means not good, thought Matthews. Perhaps he should have listened to Christine and Ron Carey.

—

At about 7:55 Matthews stood outside the Iroquois to wait for Julia to pick him up as planned. Under his top coat he wore his new bone button blazer and a smart Ralph Lauren tie. He tried not to pace by leaning slightly on the handrail accompanying the steps to the entrance of the hotel. By nature, Matthews enjoyed taking chances, and he was not afraid to make decisions where success was not guaranteed. He found himself inexplicably eager to become involved with the Schmidhausen family when he could have exercised restraint to wait for more information. However, Matthews found Agnes and Julia Schmidhausen to be convincingly guileless, and in fact, he was intrigued by both women. Nevertheless, he found the absence of information about Julia on the Hunter website to be troubling.

A black Lincoln Town Car pulled up promptly at 8:00 p.m. The driver jumped out and ran around the car to open the back door for Matthews. Matthews looked into the back seat of the car which was illuminated by the ceiling light. He almost didn't recognize Julia. Her coat was folded on the seat next to her, and she was wearing a long dark burgundy dress, the lines of which were unclear to Matthews because she was seated. The dress revealed her ankles, and her shoes had very high heels; how high was something Matthews was inexperienced at estimating. Her hair was held up in the back by a tortoise shell comb and her neck looked long and graceful, like that of a ballet dancer.

"Garth, I am so grateful you are coming with me."

Matthews climbed into the car where he could see Julia's face in the dim light. For the second time in one day he was surprised by her appearance. He immediately wondered how he could have ever thought her face was plain. Her glasses were gone. Her eye make-up was applied in a way that empha-sized her Asian features, and her skin, which had looked rather ordinary in Le Cheval Blanc, had an iridescence that was evident even in the dim light of the car. Matthews' feelings were pinned between a buoyancy to be with such a beautiful woman and a fear that she could be a complete, possibly danger-ous, charlatan.

The driver returned to his seat, and the car headed to the Upper West Side. Matthews was so tortured by his conflicted feelings that he felt he had to resolve them before the evening progressed.

"Julia, I looked for you on the Hunter website, and I couldn't find you. To be honest, I was curious where you had studied."

"What name did you use for your search?"

"Julia Schmidhausen."

"You wouldn't find me under the name of Schmidhausen. My family did not start using the name again until I was in my late twenties at about the time when the current foundation was created. Because of the family activities during the war, they had been persecuted by the Nazis. The family used its fortune to assist Jews in escaping from Nazis persecution, and the family actually used a variety of names for decades depending upon the county we were in. I would love to tell you the history of my family when we have more time."

"So, what surname do you use?"

"I received my degrees under the name of Julia Nghiem. So that's how I am known in academic circles. Here, Garth, let me show you."

Julia reached into her purse. Matthews thought she would show him her Hunter I.D. card, but instead she pulled out her I-Phone. She quickly found the Hunter website and searched for her name.

"Here Garth. Look," she said in a way that was devoid of any defensiveness.

Matthews took the I-Phone and scrolled through the information about Professor Julia Nghiem: Bachelor of Arts from Harvard College; Masters and Doctorate in Art History from Yale; two fellowships at the Sorbonne; an internship at the Louvre. These were unquestionably Julia's credentials because her web page included her picture. She was no imposter with counterfeit credentials. Hardly. She was a remarkably accomplished woman.

Matthews became apologetic, something that was not entirely necessary. But his balance had been thrown off by so many sudden changes in his life, and he felt badly that he considered the possibility that Julia was a fraud. "I am sorry. I just had to ask you. The possibility of receiving such a large cash award seems somewhat surreal. It has made me want to investigate the authenticity of everything connected with it."

"I understand that an award like this can have a profound effect on a person. It's completely normal. You wouldn't be human if it didn't affect you."

Matthews found her words and her soothing tone very comforting. And released from his fear that Julia was a fraud, he became euphoric to be in the company of a woman who not only was exquisitely beautiful but also extraordinarily sensitive.

The Town Car arrived at the Upper East Side destination. The doorman at the building told Julia and Matthews that Posse resided on the sixteenth floor. As they rode up the elevator, Julia reached for Matthews' hand, and with a gentle squeeze, she thanked him again for accompanying her.

"I can't begin to tell you how awkward I would feel going to an event like this by myself. The host often tries to make me feel like I am his date, rather than just a guest."

The elevator door opened to a party that was well underway. The guests were talking loudly, and the odor was boozy and smoky. Except for the guests' contemporary attire, the whole image was very East Egg, Gatsbyesque. A gentleman in the entrance hall of Posse's residence took Matthews' and Julia's coats, and another man appeared with a tray of glasses of champagne. Julia took a glass, and Matthews declined in the hope that there would be Scotch inside.

The marble entrance hall led to a living room that would be considered enormous even if it were located in a mansion on the North Shore of Long Island. In fact, the room was so cavernous that marble columns were structurally necessary to create such a large volume of space in the twenty-two story building. There were oversized oil paintings on the walls, most of which were proportionate to the oversized windows

The room was filled seemingly to capacity with guests, most of whom were more casually dressed than Matthews and Julia. Matthews spotted a gentleman with a tray of Martinis, who offered one to Matthews.

"No, thank you. Are there other choices?" asked Matthews.

"Yes, whatever you'd like."

Matthews asked for a Scotch which he was quickly provided.

As they sipped their drinks, Matthews and Julia stood closely together and anyone who wondered would readily assume they were a couple.

"I'm sorry that I asked you to wear a jacket. I had no idea that the men would be so casually dressed."

"That's okay. Your dress is really magnificent. At least with a jacket and tie, I look like I could be your date. Besides, my guiding principle for fashion is simple: Always dress like you're going somewhere better afterward."

Julia noticeably suppressed a laugh and almost choked on her champagne. Matthews smiled at the thought that he caught her off guard and made her laugh.

"Are any of these paintings Old Masters? Frankly, you can teach me a great deal about art."

"No, these are mostly Nineteenth Century paintings and American paintings. None of them are really that valuable to a real collector. For one thing they are mostly too large to be Old Masters. Old Masters are usually not this large, but there are exceptions. You know most people are surprised by the small size of the Mona Lisa."

"Yes, I have heard that."

"Also, this room has too many windows for hanging Old Masters. Of course, they could be covered by the day, or the windows could have room darkening shades, but most private owners of valuable art have dedicated rooms to house their collections. It's odd that Posse has these paintings in his living room. They are not bad paintings, but they are bourgeois when compared to the really valuable art he claims to have somewhere here."

"Do you see Posse?"

"Well, I only met him briefly; I'm not sure I will recognize him. Let's mingle, and look for someone who seems a bit creepy."

"I think there are a lot of candidates. That doesn't narrow the field much for me."

They made their way around the periphery of the room, appearing to be interested in the artwork on the walls. Julia took Matthews' arm, something which pleased him immensely. They nodded politely at the other guests and chatted briefly with a young couple who seemed very upper crusty. In the brief conversation, Julia and Matthews learned that neither of them had to work for a living and that they lived on Long Island in a house on Sands Point, overlooking Manhasset Bay.

At about the fourth painting, a bald, slender man with pale skin and round glasses rudely and clumsily pushed through the guests to approach Matthews and Julia.

"Professor Nghiem. I am so glad you could make it."

Julia gently squeezed Matthews' arm to signal that this was Posse. Indeed, thought Matthews, this guy's creepiness is prizeworthy.

"I didn't know you would be accompanied by someone," said Posse with a disappointment in his voice that made him all the more disturbing.

"Yes, this is Garth Matthews. Garth is in town from Chicago. He is Dean of the Law School at Lortigue University." Posse seemed to take some comfort in the fact that Matthews had a prestigious academic position.

"I shall have to introduce you to some of the guests. They will be impressed that I know people from academia. And before it gets too late, Professor and Dean, let me show you the paintings that I mentioned to Professor Nghiem after her lecture. It will be a quick tour for now, because I don't want to leave the guests for very long. But you are welcome to come back when we can spend more time."

The latter comment was obviously directed exclusively to Julia.

Posse led Matthews and Julia around the perimeter of the room to a hallway at the other side of the room. Posse stopped along the way to introduce them to other guests, always emphasizing Matthews' and Julia's academic titles.

When they reached the hallway, there was a small table about half way down the corridor where Posse set down his drink. It was obvious to Matthews and Julia that they should do the same. At the end of the hallway, there was an elevator which Posse accessed by placing his palm on an illuminated screen. A light passed under his hand from beneath the screen, a green light quickly glared brightly on the device, and the elevator door opened. The three entered the elevator. Once inside, Posse placed his right hand on a similar palm recognition device and simultaneously pushed the "up" button with his left hand. The elevator car moved smoothly, and the door opened to a dimly lit room no bigger than ten feet square. Posse turned up the lighting to reveal what appeared to be a desk with a number of switches, dials and computer screens inlaid flat into the surface of the table.

"Of course," said Posse, "We carefully control the temperature, barometric pressure and humidity in the gallery that houses the collection."

Matthews and Julia nodded as if to say, "Of course."

Posse made some adjustments on the devices on the desk and flipped several switches with an intensity that appeared he was about to launch a missile. The door at the end of the room opposite the elevator slid open, revealing the beginning of a labyrinth of corridors that made the maximum use of wall space to hang the collection. Posse grandly gestured that Matthews and Julia should enter the gallery.

It was clear from the beginning of the tour, that Posse was not concerned about providing Matthews and Julia with the opportunity to linger and appreciate each piece. He was much more intent on impressing them, particularly Julia, with his acquisitions. He repeatedly told Julia that she should come back when he had more time, something that Matthews thought she would never let happen if she had to be alone in this space with Posse. Matthews was very glad that he had accompanied Julia to Posse's home because he was certain that Julia would have felt extremely uncomfortable to be alone in this confined space with Posse. Matthews thought that Posse was really harmless, but the sheer discomfort of being alone with such a repellant person would be an experience that any rational person would want to avoid. Matthews detected that he felt very protective of Julia, and he was not sure why.

Posse led Matthews and Julia through the corridors of the gallery at a steady pace; announcing the names of well-known painters as they passed their works: Degas, Bellini, Rembrandt, Signorelli, Ruben, Renoir and then, names that Matthews did not recognize. While Matthews knew that his appreciation of these masterpieces could not match that of Julia, he was irritated by their host's rudeness and his lack of respect for artwork that commanded more than a passing glimpse. He felt badly that Julia was not being afforded the opportunity to appreciate the art unless she returned, as Posse repeatedly invited her to do. Once he caught on to Posse's gambit, he started to walk slowly and lag behind. Occasionally, he would stop and stare at a painting as if entranced. And when Posse would try to hurry him along, Matthews would ask a question as to some feature on the painting. Julia quickly caught on to Matthews' clever ability to take control of the situation, and she could barely suppress a smile when she made eye contact with him. Posse was becoming increasing agitated, and Matthews responded by repeatedly telling him how impressed he was with the collection and how gracious Posse was to show them such extraordinary art. Ultimately, Posse stated that he had to get back to the guests.

Matthews then asked what he knew to be a perfectly ridiculous question, but he could not resist, "Would you mind if we just linger a bit up here in the gallery. I'm sure Julia would love…"

"No. I just don't handle the gallery that way. I, ah…" Posse began stumbling over his words.

Matthews decided to push his counter-gambit one more step, more for Julia's amusement than anything else. "Well, surely you trust Professor Nghiem with your collection." Julia obviously enjoyed watching Matthews skillfully disarm such a boorish host.

Posse was at a loss for words, but being the chivalrous combatant that he was, Matthews looked at his watch, and said, "Oh Julia, we are going to be late. We must be going. I am sorry, Mr. Posse. We are expected at the French Ambassador's home for dinner. We are really quite late." Matthews took Julia by the hand, ran through the maze of the gallery and into the elevator, which of course, could not be moved without Posse's palm print.

Joining in the fun, Julia cried out to Posse, "Please hurry. We are very late. Hurry." She looked at Matthews with a smile of a young child who was winning a secret game.

As they were riding down the elevator, Julia continued to be playful, "Mr. Posse, you have been such a marvelous host. We should have never tried to fit this in before such an important social event. Please, when we get off the elevator, could you find our coats while I call for our driver? I do hope they are not holding dinner for us."

When they exited the elevator, Posse ran down the corridor, screaming for one of his staff to bring the coats. Amidst some commotion, the coats appeared which Matthews grabbed on the run to the door. Once the door closed on the elevator to the lobby, Matthews and Julia burst into laughter.

"Garth, that was masterful," She said while catching her breath from laughing convulsively "I can't remember when I laughed so hard. Does the French Ambassador live in New York?"

"No. I am quite sure that he lives in Washington, D. C."

"That makes it even funnier."

When they walked out of the lobby of Posse's building, the car was not in sight.

"You didn't call for the car?" asked Matthews.

"No. There is a lovely restaurant about two blocks from here. They know me, so we shouldn't have any trouble getting a table. My treat."

"That's not fair. Can't I treat you like you're my date? We are not still doing business, are we?"

"Oh, you are my date, no question about that. I expect a kiss good night when the date ends. I think I am entitled to that."

Matthews smiled at the charming way Julia had of letting him know that she liked him without appearing awkwardly aggressive.

"Then, I will pick up the check. That's what a guy does on the first date."

Julia took Matthews' arm, and they walked to the restaurant.

The maître d' hotel at Chamard's did know Julia, and she and Matthews were immediately seated at a corner table where there was minimal light and the opportunity for private conversation. Matthews asked for a wine list, and after consultation with Julia, he ordered a Chateau Angelus St. Emilion Grand Cru, a red French Bordeaux from 2003. The sommelier complimented him on his selection. Matthews figured that for anything over one hundred dollars a bottle, there should be a compliment.

Matthews and Julia were still in a playful mood after their visit to Posse's gallery.

"You don't think I was mean to him?" asked Matthews.

"No. Not at all. His behavior was absolutely ill-mannered. Occasionally, people like that need to be confronted. Besides, you were extremely entertaining."

Julia laughed just thinking about their exit and their dash past the other guests, with coats flying.

"Now you deserve to be entertained." She reached in her purse and pulled out four Vietnamese coins and a deck of cards. "Now we'll see one of the reasons my father called me Bion."

"Fortune telling or a magic trick?"

"Magic, if you have the patience. I am actually researching a project about the poster art of early Twentieth Century magicians. It also involves actual oil portraits, some of which are quite well done. There are also pieces of magical apparatus that might be considered a step above folk art. But what really makes them remarkable is the exquisite paintings on the apparatus, frequently a portrait of the magician's assistant. It is believed that some of these props were disassembled and hung as wall art."

"Where is this stuff?"

"It's probably not in the United States. Some of it could be in St. Petersburg, but I would guess that most of it is in Berlin and Vienna. Hitler had his favorite magicians, none of whom ever acknowledged that their magic was trickery rather than sorcery. In Hitler's private library, the subject most represented above all others was sorcery."

"Please show me something," said Matthews, gesturing to the cards and coins.

Julia placed the coins in a square, with each coin about eight inches from the other. She covered each coin with a card. Julia then proceeded to have coins jump invisibly so that by the time she finished, all four coins were under just one card.

"That's called a 'matrix.' It is a rather common trick, but not many people do it really well."

"That was definitely sorcery, not trickery. I have no idea how you did that. What else can you show me?"

Julia shuffled the full deck of cards and asked Matthews to do the same after handing the deck to him. Julia asked him to select a card, and if he didn't like it, he could return it and select another. Julia then took a Sharpie marker from her purse and asked Matthews to sign his name across the face of the card.

"Are you sure you want me to sign the card; it will ruin the deck."

"Well, it won't be much of a trick if you don't."

Matthews signed the card, the two of hearts, and placed it on top of the deck. Julia showed him the signed card one more time and then handed it to Matthews and asked him to insert it anywhere in the middle of the deck.

Julia did not touch the deck, but snapped her fingers above the cards. "Done. Please pick up the top card on the deck."

Matthews did as he was told, and the card with his signature had traveled from the middle of the deck to the top.

"Bravo. That was 100% sorcery."

"That's called the 'Ambitious Card.' I guess it is called that because the card starts in the middle of the pack and ambitiously makes its way to the top. I suppose that's like some ambitious people. There is a bit of deception along the way to the top. It's a favorite among magicians. Here, the card is your souvenir."

"Thank you. You sign it as well. And it wouldn't hurt if you would put your telephone number on the card too. Could you teach me a few tricks?"

"Of course. But there is a condition: I wouldn't teach you a trick just so you could learn the method. That would be completely contrary to the art of magic. It is an art, you know, just like painting. I would only teach you a trick if you promised to practice it and perform it. You can even come with me to magic club meetings where they have lectures."

"Do you do that regularly? Attend magic club meetings?"

"Yes. I like magicians. They are interesting people, and they represent a variety of backgrounds: doctors, sales people, and professors. Some of the clubs are affiliated with national organizations, but some are just informal groups that get together for lunch. These people usually meet at a magic shop, like Lou Tannen's."

"Would you take me there some time – Lou Tannen's?"

"Yes, of course."

The waiter brought the menu and apprised Julia and Matthews of the specials. The wine arrived, and the sommelier decanted it.

"Julia, tell me about Posse's collection. I realize we didn't have time to study it, but you must have been able to recognize some paintings."

"Actually, I was able to identify almost everything that was there. I have a trained eye, and I have spent the good portion of my waking hours looking at paintings."

"Tell me about what he has."

"Where should I start? Well, first he has a tremendously valuable collection. The value of any single authentic Grand Master could easily be worth millions of dollars, and he has several. But his collection, I don't believe, could ever be sold for its real value."

"Why is that?"

"With the exception of a few pieces, most of the art in Posse's gallery appears to have been obtained through questionable channels. If one of those pieces were put on the open market, it would likely be confiscated and returned to the rightful owner, or more likely to the owner's descendants. Actually, some of what I saw was probably once owned by countries like France and Russia."

"You really are amazing if you could pick up all that by merely glancing at the paintings."

"Well, Garth, I have had a lot of training. It is what I do in my career. But I am also lucky, because I have a God given photographic memory. I could memorize the entire sequence of that deck of cards just by flipping through it. I am a savant, I guess. What this all means, however, is that given my academic training, if I have seen a reasonable high resolution photograph of a piece of art, I can remember every detail. And I can even remember the details of brush strokes from an artist in one painting and identify them in a distinct painting."

"That's amazing. Are there many people who have this talent?"

"There are lots of people who have photographic memories for visual images, but I don't believe they have the academic training I have. So, you could say that I have a unique skill."

"Well, tell me. If Posse's paintings were originally stolen, and could not be acquired, say, at an auction at Christie's or Sotheby's, where did he get them?"

"Collectors have been known to commission a theft. That's unlikely, but it happens. You have heard of the theft of the Edvard Munch works?"

"Yes, of course."

"But the person who has possession of recently stolen artwork can do no more than privately enjoy the work. If he were to use it as a form of currency, its worth would be vastly diminished if not nonexistent."

"There was a major theft in Boston in the early 90's, wasn't there?"

"Yes. The Gardner Museum. But actually, I saw nothing in Posse's collection that I could identify as recently stolen art. In fact, in my life I haven't seen any."

"Well then, where did he get his collection?"

"Regrettably, there is a huge underground international market for stolen art, and its origin may surprise you. The vast majority of this art was not obtained through some heist, but rather, it has been circulating in this phantom market since World War II. The people who buy and sell this art are well known to one another, particularly in the United States. Through this market a buyer can obtain a masterpiece at a fraction of the price that the rightful owner would demand for it."

"What type of person does this?"

"You would be amazed at the type of people who deal in this underground market. Many are otherwise respectable people who really don't fully understand the impropriety of what they are doing. But actually, most of them know that there is something fishy, but they just don't know exactly what it is. It's the ones who buy and sell this stuff in an effort to make a large profit who are really corrupt."

"Do you think that Posse just buys this stuff, or is he in the business of buying and selling?"

"I would guess that he started out just buying, but it's more exciting for these people to be both buyers and sellers."

"But how did this market get supplied in the first place?"

The waiter apparently thought he saw a break in the conversation and approached the table. Julia and Matthews hastily ordered from the menu in order to quickly return to Julia's explanation of the creation of the underground market.

"When a scholar studies art history, he or she almost inevitably studies the fate of art during the Second World War. Now you'll have to forgive me if this sounds somewhat like a classroom lecture. That's because it is. Maybe some of the wine will make my delivery less dry."

Matthews filled her glass. "Don't worry. I find this intriguing. Let's not forget that we are both academics. Our dates always involve conversations about some cerebral topic. Okay, I am curious about the World War II connection."

"I'll try to simplify it as much as possible because frankly, this lecture usually takes three sessions. Well, as you know, the greatest concentration of valuable art in the 1930's and 1940's was in a number of European cities: Paris, Rome, Berlin, Vienna and a few others. All of these cities were directly impacted by the war. A number of major forces had the effect of disrupting rightful ownership of art during this period.

"First, Hitler considered himself a connoisseur of the arts, and he wanted to acquire art of all types from the occupied cities. He attempted to bring all of this plundered art to Paris, at the Museum Jeu de Paune. He ultimately wanted this art transported to his birthplace of Linsk where he intended to create an enormous museum complex. Much of the art never made it to Paris, but rather was looted by German officers for their private collections. Goering himself was the worst offender.

"The second cause was the fact that the major art centers of Europe were well aware of Hitler's intentions, and before the Nazi occupation could occur, there was an effort in most of these cities to remove the valuable art from the museums to remote, hidden locations. Some of this art has shown up years later in a barn or a cave. The process was very rushed, and there is no way that any real inventory could be kept."

"Is this art still around today in these hiding places?"

"Yes, occasionally there will be a report of a land owner finding a piece of valuable art in a well or an abandoned mine."

"Interesting."

"Finally, during the post-war recovery effort, there was looting by allied forces despite an attempt by the United States to collect the German plundered artwork at a 'Central Collection Point' in Munich. A special team organized by the United States sought to protect the art, and they even used subterfuge. For example, they used land mine field flags to keep looters away." Julia continued, "To understand the full picture, you have to keep in mind that a valuable painting could be easily cut from its frame, rolled and tucked into a ten-inch cardboard tube. That tube can then become a form of currency worth millions of dollars."

Matthews was extremely impressed by Julia's capability of looking so incredibly beautiful while performing sorcery, and then so cogently explaining a critical episode in art history.

"Julia," said Matthews, reaching for her hand across the table, "you are a remarkable woman. I truly mean that. We are still on a date, aren't we?"

"Well, yes."

Matthews turned his head slightly and leaned across the table, and Julia reciprocated. He kissed her lightly on the check and squeezed her hand gently.

"Good. This is certainly a very fine date." An image of Christine's frowning face suddenly flashed in Matthews' mind, but it was quickly gone.

When their dinner concluded, Matthews paid the check as he had previously insisted. The Town Car was waiting for them outside of Chamard's. The driver was dozing, and Julia tapped on the window which resulted in what appeared to be an automatic response of seamless actions by the driver of straightening his cap, jumping out of the car, and opening the door for Julia. Matthews let himself in the car once the doors were unlocked.

"Where do you live?" asked Matthews, once they were settled in the car.

"I live on the upper East side, near where we had lunch. It's a greystone. I like the location because I can walk to my office."

"Do you have valuable art on the walls?"

"No, not really." Then possibly changing the subject, but possibly not, Julia's tone turned flirtatious, "Garth, you didn't insist on paying for dinner because you want to sleep with me tonight?"

Matthews was completely surprised by the question, and he couldn't tell if she was being serious or playful. He tried not to sound defensive. "Truthfully, Julia, I never even considered the possibility that we would spend the night together." He was, in fact, telling the truth.

"What if I told you I am disappointed? Actually, I am, but I would never let myself stay with you. I am much too shy for that." Julia's candor was totally unexpected, even to her.

"I wouldn't say you are shy. You have too much self-confidence. I can't imagine you being shy about anything. I would say you are cautious and conservative. But I do get a second date, don't I?"

"Of course. Will you have breakfast with me before you leave New York tomorrow?"

"Absolutely," replied Matthews, without hesitation.

"Well, if that's the case, we can have a virtual sleepover. I was sort of planning on it."

"A virtual sleepover?"

"It's everything like sleeping together without the sex and the sleeping together. I have already had my things sent to the Iroquois. I have a room on the seventh floor. When we get to the hotel, we'll both put on something more comfortable, and I'll come to your suite. We can order a night cap. Later, you will walk me home to the seventh floor, and I will call you in the morning when I wake up. We can have breakfast in your suite or we can go out. How does that sound?"

"It actually sounds quite nice. And I think it is within the ground rules laid out by your grandmother."

Julia laughed, because she knew what Agnes had planned to say to Matthews about his tallywacker.

The Town Car took them to the Iroquois, and Julia went to the front desk to get her key card.

"I'll be just a few minutes. Just put on some jeans or casual slacks."

Matthews did as he was instructed and waited patiently in his room. After Julia arrived and sat on the couch, Matthews sat in a chair with several feet of space between them in order to demonstrate that he was a man who could be trusted with the etiquette of a virtual sleepover. He was absolutely certain that he would not violate the boundaries of the 'virtual' nature of the sleepover, but he found himself craving the idea of intimacy with Julia. He hadn't felt these longings for a very long time. Not with Christine. Not with anyone since the death of his wife. In fact, he momentarily wondered whether he could trust Julia because she was just so incredibly beguiling. But the thought was only fleeting, and he decided that mobilizing his defenses would be completely unnecessary and foolish.

Julia was wearing jeans and a faded sweatshirt, though a different one than the Hunter sweatshirt she wore during lunch. She had removed the comb from her hair, and her hair, definitely black, seemed even longer than it did at lunch. Again, Matthews marveled at the notion that he once thought of her as plain. He tried to explain it to himself, but he could not.

"What can I order for you?" said Matthews, reaching for the room service menu.

"I brought this small bottle of pinot noir from the mini bar in my room." She reached in her oversized purse and pulled out the bottle.

"We do have wine glasses somewhere. I'll have a Scotch. In fact you should take this bottle with you. It was a gift from the manager, and I can't take it on the plane."

With drinks in hand, they each resumed their prior places. A feeling of total privacy and safety came over both of them, and Matthews began to understand the benefits of a virtual sleepover. For both Matthews and Julia, there was also a peaceful feeling in knowing that the date would end without any awkward doubts about sleeping together. So many times in Matthews' life, his dates became an exercise of decoding encrypted statements by women who were trying to tell him that they did or did not want to have sex with him.

Julia began the conversation. "Garth, you know this cash award, as large as it may be, will not change you. It will just make certain things in your life easier to accomplish. It will also give you more time to do things you really want to do."

"How do you know it won't change me?"

"Well, the selection process for the Schmidhausen Award is really quite extensive. I have not been kidding you when I have told you I know a great deal about you. In fact one of the assessments that a Schmidhausen referee must make is a determination of whether the cash award will alter the values of the recipient."

"But you don't know everything about me, not really. There are so many parts of my life that are known only to me: my fears; my disappointments; my frustrations; my simple pleasures. There are parts of myself that even I don't understand."

Julia looked down as if she lost confidence in what she was saying. "You're right, of course. Actually, there is a part of me that truly wishes I did know everything about you." She looked up and smiled winsomely. "But you do kind of come with an owner's manual. And while I don't know everything about you, the documentation is considerably more than I will ever have on any other man. The dossier has actually given me a sense of self-confidence and a sense of safety that I haven't had with other men. I am usually not a good date. I am quiet. And I really am shy. But you see, I felt I knew you and liked you well before we met. It was such an adolescent feeling, I knew that I couldn't take it seriously. But honestly, I couldn't help it. I even fantasized about our lunch together before it happened."

"Did it live up to your fantasy?"

"Oh, yes. Yes. It far exceeded my fantasy. I was so afraid I wouldn't have the courage to ask you to go with me to the party tonight, but when the time came to ask, the words came easily. I was truly afraid that you would turn me down not because you had other commitments, but because you weren't interested in spending time with me."

Matthews was both touched and mildly surprised. Emotionally, he felt he was able to empathize with what Julia was telling him. Matthews believed that everyone suffered from some shyness and that it was a healthy and even an appealing attribute. The trick, he believed, was never to excessively over-compensate because it always resulted in overbearing behavior.

Julia continued, "All day since lunch, I have had this fear that you would call and cancel our date. Please don't misunderstand, these are not pathological feelings. But they make me understand things about myself."

Matthews immediately wanted to reassure her about the connection he felt with her, but that would be completely unfair. There are so few real assurances in a relationship, especially one that is less than twelve hours old. But he wanted to tell her that for him, the evening had become much more than a social obligation. "Julia, I can tell you this: We will have other dates, I promise. And now I do understand something about having resources. The cost of flying between New York and Chicago seems suddenly immaterial."

"See, I told you. Having the means to do something that you really want to do is a wonderful benefit of having money. To be truthful, I have had the money to do whatever I wanted in life, and it has not made me lazy. In my career, it has enabled me to see artwork that a typical art history professor would not have the financial ability to see. I have been able to travel to all the major art centers, and it has made me a better professor."

"But Julia, your shyness surprises me. Where does this shyness come from? You really are a very accomplished person."

"Of course it's complex. Mainly I can easily conceal my shyness because I am so practiced at speaking to people. As a professor, I frequently have classes in large lecture halls with over a hundred students. So except in certain kinds of situations, like dating, no one ever sees the shyness. It's like a magic trick; it involves deception," she said with a slight shrug.

"But that doesn't explain where the shyness comes from in the first place."

"I think that much of the shyness, especially with men, is an innate part of my upbringing. I was raised in a very strict family, and I was an only child. I went to girls' academies until college, and I was not allowed really to date until I was in college. There were supervised events that I was permitted to attend with a boy, but there was no dating without a chaperone. Interestingly, I never had the desire to rebel. It felt safer that way.

"In college I dated, but I really did not have any serious relationships. Guys just sensed I was shy and studious. I looked younger than my age, and I think most boys wanted to be seen with girls who looked like women. The guys who asked me out just didn't appeal to me, but in graduate school, I had one, rather short, relationship. One day, however, the guy just disappeared. He stopped calling. That was it. I was hurt, but I never had the feeling he was the one. The experience just made me very cautious. It was a lesson I should have learned much earlier in life. Guys can just vanish on you.

"When I became a professor, I looked so young, students would ask me out. Of course, I didn't want to date college boys. There were some professors I dated, but nothing ever seriously developed until I met this guy, Kevin Arthur. He was a political science professor. He said he was attracted to me because I looked so young. You don't have to be a psychiatrist to know that this is a very bad danger sign. But I didn't see it. I was so self-conscious about my appearance that I was flattered. I liked him because he would always say the right things. In fact, he was incredibly clever at it, and he made me feel good about myself. But, in actuality, he said the right things because he was a skilled liar. The relationship became increasingly controlling and abusive, until I realized what was happening. He insisted on knowing where I was at any moment, and he expected me to be with him whenever he demanded. He would become crazy when he didn't know where I was. When he felt he was losing control of me, he became even more possessive. He stalked me, and it ended with an ugly two days of being locked in his bedroom. That's where I found photographs of me that I had no idea had been taken. This wasn't the first time in his life he had acted this way. His whole life, including his academic credentials, had been a fraud. Fortunately, he is not scheduled to be released from the Ithaca Correctional Institution for several years."

"How long ago was that?"

"About five years ago. I think that if I had a more conventional dating life before I met him, I would have detected signals immediately that would have scared me away. Well, I haven't had a serious relationship since then."

"Five years. That's about how long it's been for me, being in a serious relationship that is."

"What does it mean for you to be in a serious relationship?"

"I am not sure I have established criteria," Matthews said with a smile. "One day I would just realize that I was in a relationship that seemed serious and monogamous. I know you didn't ask this, but I will tell you. I've never had sex with a woman until we were dating for a long time. I wish I could give you some principled reason for it, and I am sure there are many, but I was in a good marriage when my wife suddenly died. Maybe it's patterned or conditioned, but I wouldn't feel comfortable about having sex with someone I really didn't know."

"But Garth, you have power. You take care of yourself. I am sure you could…"

"I know what you are saying. And for a while, three years after my wife died, I dated quite a bit. Chicago has a lot of single people, and, of course, I was younger. But after a while I realized I just didn't like it. Dating with the purpose of finding a lifetime partner is exhausting and seemingly futile. And one part of it I really didn't like at all is that many women, at least those I dated, believed that the way to keep a man is to sleep with him. It was very awkward at times. I guess I just wasn't ready for it. It just didn't feel that it was a way to find someone with whom I would want to spend the rest of my life. I just always felt that someone should invent a better system."

"And the serious relationships?"

"There were two, and they were shorter than you might expect. Maybe unlike you, I could pick up on the warning signals in a relatively short period of time. Also, I just felt there was something missing. It wasn't some small matter that I could overlook. I think it was the absence of any real feeling of a connection. But equally possible, I just wasn't ready, and the lack of connection and the warning signs were benignly of my own making. Looking back, I really couldn't say."

Matthews and Julia paused and took a moment to just look at one another. A broad smile simultaneously came over each of their faces. They simply stared at one another for seemingly a matter of minutes with neither feeling any sense of awkwardness.

"Garth," said Julia breaking the silence." "I actually know an extraordinary amount of information about you. Tell me something I might not know."

"Well," replied Matthews. "I actually enjoy taking risks, the kind that would keep me from becoming complacent."

"Do you mean bungee jumping and skydiving, things like that?"

"Oh, no. I would never do those sorts of things. I'm not a dare devil or thrill seeker. I'm talking about taking chances with the path of my life and career: The type of things that would keep me from becoming numb from the predictability of life."

"Can you give me some examples?"

"You actually know of most of the things I have done in my life, but maybe you didn't understand the motivation behind them. Let's see. Actually, when I agreed to be the founding dean of the law school at Lortigue, that involved one of the greatest professional risks of my career. I left the safety of a tenured position at the University of Cincinnati, where I was comfortable."

"And complacent?" interjected Julia.

"Exactly: Comfortable and complacent. Creating a law school out of nothingness, however, involves taking one risk after another without any real guarantee of success. The 'Big Bang Theory' doesn't apply to law schools. They must be created by taking one step after another. And every step involves a risk. A major misstep can doom the whole enterprise. The early years in creating the College of Law were, well, extremely exhilarating. Every day was a new challenge. I think it was during those first five years that I learned that I was happiest when I was being tested. After the law school became accredited by the American Bar Association and was recognized as an established institution, there were new, more nuanced challenges. They were not as exciting as those of the first few years, but still very important in achieving the current success of the law school. When I look back, I realize how big the risk of failure actually was, but when we were first building the law school, I never gave failure a thought."

"That does put your decision to leave Cincinnati into perspective. Any other examples?" asked Julia, fascinated by this new insight into Matthews' psyche.

"The other episodes pale in comparison to being the founding dean at Lortigue. They involved things like serving on a State Department Commission which evaluated the relevance of legal education to the actual practice of law in Iraq."

"The risk?"

"I had to visit Baghdad three times."

"I guess that qualifies as involving risk."

"Other things were small in scope and more subtle as to the risk. Looking back, I have sought out adventures that just involved the possible waste of time, like hosting a syndicated talk show for sale to European markets. I taped sixteen episodes interviewing successful European entrepreneurs who decided to live in the United States. The series sold well in Europe, but it was never aired in the States. I did it just for the experience, for the adventure. It could have been a complete flop, but thankfully for my self-esteem, it wasn't."

"I actually knew about the State Department Commission, and I do recall that you were involved with the television show. You are a remarkable person."

Matthews decided not to disclose to Julia that he was a highly ranked Texas Hold'em player and that he regularly participated in high stakes tournaments. It was a fact that he did his best to conceal from the legal education community and everyone at Lortigue University except George and Jean Lortigue. The Lortigues were also world class Texas Hold'em players and had introduced Matthews to the game. Matthews avoided tournaments that might receive national attention, but when life became particularly uninspiring, he would fly off to Las Vegas for a weekend of excitement.

Julia continued, "Why do you think you take these risks, not that they aren't admirable."

"I am not entirely sure. I could simply say that I need excitement, but of course, it's more complicated than that. It might have something to do with filling an emptiness that I sometimes feel. Possibly boredom. I really don't know."

"Well, let's talk about it more. I would like to understand you better." Changing the subject, Julia said, "Garth, I am a late sleeper on Sundays, but I can get up early if you have a morning flight."

"Actually, I have an open ticket. The flights to Chicago leave every few hours on Sundays. You can sleep as late as you like. Just call me when you wake up."

"You are going to walk me to my room aren't you?"

"Of course. And I know I have a promise to fulfill."

As they walked to the elevator and then to Julia's room, Matthews wondered how such a shy person could have mustered the courage to commit him to a kiss. He did not worry about it long, and when they reached her room, he kissed her gently on the mouth, ensuring that Julia received full performance of their contract. Matthews actually wanted to kiss Julia more passionately, but he was afraid if he did, Julia might interpret his behavior as an effort to elicit an invitation to join her in her room. As much as the prospect of making love with Julia excited him, he had a much stronger desire to gain her trust. Besides, he had given his word.

Matthews walked back to the elevator feeling confident that he handled the kiss rather well. He was definitely enjoying this adventure.

CHAPTER SIX

SUNDAY

MATTHEWS AWOKE AT ABOUT 7:00, worked out in the health club, and ordered coffee once back at his suite. He was about one third of his way through the Sunday New York Times when his phone rang. It was Julia.

"Good morning Garth, I just woke up. I can be ready in about half an hour."

"That's fine. I am just reading the paper. Let me ask you something: I have been trying to figure out how many dates we've had. Is it two, and breakfast is the third?"

"Don't be silly, you get credit for one date and that's it. Lunch yesterday was not a date; you get no credit for that whatsoever. And the party, dinner and the virtual sleepover count as one date."

"This must be the new math. See you in half an hour," he said with a smile in his voice.

Just short of thirty minutes later, Julia knocked on Matthews' door.

"I have already checked out. My things are with the bellman. Let's go out for breakfast; it's actually warm for March, and we can walk afterward."

At breakfast, Julia looked even more alluring than the night before, even though she was casually dressed and her makeup was minimal. Matthews marveled at Julia's ability to look more beautiful every time he saw her. The phenomenon was unlike anything Matthews had experienced before.

After they ordered from the menu, Garth seemed to be somewhat uneasy.

"What is it?" asked Julia.

"Last night, when you asked what I did for excitement, I failed to tell you that I am a high stakes poker player – Texas Hold'em to be more precise."

"Oh, I knew that. You can't believe that the Schmidhausen investigation would have failed to uncover that?"

"I hadn't really thought about the investigation. Anyway, I feel rather uncomfortable that I didn't disclose this to you."

"Don't feel uncomfortable. I asked you for examples, not an exhaustive list. I knew you would discuss this with me at some point."

"Well, I still feel badly about it."

"You shouldn't. The research we did on you was exhaustive. We actually found that your penchant for poker was not only interesting, but an indication of your intelligence and capacity for strategic thinking. We found with some candidates that their more secretive activities involved mistresses and prostitutes."

"Well, you would never find a record of that kind of activity in my file...."

"Of course not. You would never have been the final candidate with that sort of sordid behavior in your record. Garth, everyone needs some distraction from his or her daily routine. All of the risk-taking in your case involves socially acceptable, if not socially beneficial activities. They are nothing that you need to apologize for. Settled?"

"Settled," replied Matthews with relief in his voice. Julia had been unguarded when she shared details of her personal life with Matthews the previous evening, and he knew that he would need to reciprocate if ever they would develop any kind of genuine emotional intimacy. He was glad he had confided in Julia, and he found himself wanting to take the risks that are essential to closeness with another person. Only three people with whom he was associated were privy to his penchant for high stakes gambling: Jean and Georges, and, of course, Rose. Their knowledge was inevitable, but with Julia, the revelation was an affirmative act of choice. Matthews' behavior involved a very unusual and uncharacteristic emotional gamble. Paradoxically, Matthews was more than comfortable with taking all kinds of risks – just not those that involved his feelings.

"Garth, I have an idea: Let's visit Lou Tannen's magic shop after we finish our breakfast."

"That sounds like it would be tremendously fun. I expected that you would want to go to an art museum."

"Honestly, I have seen everything on display right now in New York. I would love to take you to the museums sometime and be your personal docent. But we would cover so little ground today, and Tannen's would be more fun."

"Are you sure that the shop will be open today? It's Sunday."

"Yes, it opens from 10:00 a.m. until 4:00 p.m. on Sundays and Saturdays. There will be a lot of young children there, because Saturdays and Sundays are days when parents bring their budding magicians to the store."

After breakfast, Matthews and Julia took a cab to West 34th Street. Matthews was surprised that no magic shop was in sight.

"Here, Garth, it's in this building," said Julia, pointing to an office building.

They took the elevator to the sixth floor where, from the hallway, Tannen's door looked like it could be the entrance to a lawyer's or accountant's office. Julia opened the door which revealed a small, crowded room. The glass counters were full of magical apparatus of every type imaginable, and the walls had shelf upon shelf of colorful magic paraphernalia. Entering, Matthews felt like he was walking into a secret chamber, the location of which was unknown to ordinary people. Young men and women behind the counters were demonstrating magic tricks to the delight of the children who knew that they could perform that very illusion if their parents could just be convinced to purchase the apparatus. Confetti flew into the air from a device that looked like a small cannon. Silks were pulled from brightly painted boxes that had previously been shown to be empty. Card tricks were performed on what appeared to be felt placements that prevented the cards from sliding around on the glass counters. Julia later told Matthews that they were called "close-up pads," and every accomplished magician had at least one.

The young men and women behind the counters, aptly known as "demonstrators," all seemed to know Julia, and they clearly had a fondness for her. They gladly allowed Julia and Matthews to move up to the counter among the youngsters in order that Matthews might be shown a trick or two. Suddenly, Matthews was in a world where he was the equal of a child.

"What kind of skills do you have?" asked one of the demonstrators of Matthews.

"I have none whatsoever. So show me something easy to do if you want me to buy it."

The demonstrator showed Matthews a stack of nickels that he covered with a brass cap. When Matthews lifted the cap, the nickels had transformed into dimes.

"Easy?" asked Matthews.

"No skill whatsoever," replied the demonstrator, smiling at Julia who returned the smile. "It is all in the showmanship."

Fifteen minutes passed, and Matthews had purchased the nickels to dimes, several card tricks using gaffed cards, and a rope trick called "The Professor's Nightmare," which enabled the magician to change the length of various pieces of examinable rope.

Matthews and Julia then enjoyed watching the youngsters, the aspiring magicians, react to the demonstrator's tricks.

Julia whispered to Matthews, "Magic is an interesting art form. Its most fundamental premise is that the magician deceives the audience. As a general matter of human behavior, people don't like to be deceived, but the challenge for the magician is to deceive the audience and make them enjoy it."

Julia was interrupted by her cell phone. "Yes. Yes, of course. I'll take a cab."

"Is anything wrong?"

"Probably not. But Agnes had one of her spells. They took her to the hospital. I'm afraid I am going to have to see her."

"Do you want me to go with you?"

"No. I think they will only let family in to see her. Actually, this fainting has been happening quite a bit lately. It's probably nothing serious. I am extremely sorry. I was so looking forward to spending the rest of the day with you."

They took the elevator to the ground floor, and Matthews hailed a cab for Julia. She hugged Matthews and hung on to him for what seemed like minutes. Then she was gone.

Matthews was extremely disappointed that he couldn't spend the rest of the day with Julia, and he felt as if he had been robbed of something valuable. But he quickly resigned himself to returning to Chicago. It was sufficiently early that if he could get a seat on a flight in the next two hours, he would have time to go to his office to catch up on matters that had accumulated in his absence.

Once at LaGuardia, he was able to get a seat on the 2:30 flight. With the one-hour time difference, Matthews figured he could be at his office by at least 4:30.

As he was finding his seat on the plane, he noticed that Art Nelson was in the first class cabin. He was not wearing a blue suit or yellow paisley tie. He smiled at Matthews, but otherwise ignored him. It's all coincidence, thought Matthews, suppressing his paranoia.

Matthews took a cab from O'Hare directly to his office at the law school. As he rode in the backseat, he recalled Julia's insightful description of magicians. In essence, they deceive you, but they make you enjoy it. He also recalled her feats of legerdemain with cards and coins and his enjoyment in watching her. He had no idea what deceitful techniques she employed to accomplish such wizardry. And he really didn't care how she did it, realizing that often the illusion is much more entertaining than the method.

Once in his office, Matthews looked over the paperwork and mail that Rose had laid out on his desk. There appeared to be no crisis on the horizon. He had kept up with his e-mail while he was in New York, and consequently, he needed to address only the recent messages.

Jeanette Cartere sent an e-mail at 1:28:

Dean Matthews,

In light of Mrs. Schmidhausen's failing health, we would like to move up the award dinner to this coming Saturday evening. Because of the short notice, it will be a small, intimate affair. Mrs. Schmidhausen's son will be in attendance, as will her granddaughter. The dinner will be at Mrs. Schmidhausen's residence in the Waldorf Towers. Please let me know at your earliest convenience whether this schedule presents a problem.

Thanking you for your cooperation,

Jeanette Cartere.

Matthews couldn't help but marvel at the sober tone of the message. It was almost as if it could not have been written by the same rather inebriated Jeanette Cartere he had encountered on Friday.

There was also a message from Julia:

Dear Garth,

Words cannot express how much I enjoyed our time together this weekend. I am only afraid that I was too forward. My grandmother was sent home from the hospital, and Mrs. Cartere is looking after her. The poor woman is just getting old. Please call me tonight. I have a favor to ask of you.

Fondly, Julia.

Matthews considered responding to the e-mail, but he thought he would just wait to express his feelings until they spoke on the phone. He checked his pocket to make certain he had the two of hearts on which Julia had written her telephone number.

There was also an e-mail from Jean Lortigue asking that Matthews call him. Matthews immediately picked up the phone and called his cell phone number.

"Jean, how are things in Miami?"

"Fine. I'll be finishing up here in a day or two, and then I will be seeing you in Chicago for the business dean's reception."

"I am looking forward to seeing you. Will Georges be coming as well?"

"Yes, I believe so. He's in London, so it won't be a terribly long flight."

"Did you find out anything about the Schmidhausens?"

"Well, I checked with all my sources, and everyone I know thinks highly of them. I was, of course, pleased to learn that Agnes is still alive. I haven't heard from her in years."

"Yes, she is very much alive, but I think her health is failing. I met her in New York. She is quite a character."

"You should have known her when she was younger. She came to the villa a few times in the early 90's. She was a huge amount of fun. She plays the piano, you know, and one night she played and the rest of us sang. I don't think we quit until after 4:00 in the morning."

"I can picture her doing that. What do you know about her grand-daughter, Julia?"

"I didn't know she had a granddaughter. I actually never knew her children, for that matter."

"Julia and I went to a Henry Posse's home on Saturday..."

"Posse? Oh my God, Garth, stay away from that guy. I know of him through some people in Berlin. I am totally surprised he is not locked up somewhere doing serious time by now. He's not a friend of this Julia, is he?"

"No. Not at all. Nothing like that."

"Well, it would be wise not to be seen in his company. You wouldn't want a photo of the two of you showing up on the social pages of The New York Times."

"I think I already figured that out."

"Good. Well, I will see you on Tuesday night."

"See you then."

"In the meantime, I'll see if I can find out anything about the granddaughter."

"Thanks."

At his office, Matthews made as much progress as possible on the matters that had accumulated in his absence. He sent a few e-mails to Associate Deans, and left some files on Rose's desk that needed her attention. He packed up his business case and left for home.

Were it not for Rose's carefully prepared lists and notes, Matthews would have felt that his absence from the office might result in the neglect of some important matters. But Matthews traveled frequently to attend professional meetings and to meet with potential donors. Over the years, he and Rose had developed protocols for dealing with his absence which all but guaranteed that nothing would go awry.

The cab let him off at his row house, and he walked up the steps, business case in one hand and overnight bag in the other, slightly fatigued by the intensity of the weekend. Once inside, he picked up the mail off of the floor that had accumulated in the vestibule. Mail slots, he thought, are wonderful inventions; it is almost never necessary to put a hold on the mail.

He checked the refrigerator for leftovers, and while he found some, they were in a questionable state, leaning more to spoilage than edibility. He called a Thai restaurant for a delivery, and then prepared himself for the ritual of the single malt Scotch: three ice cubes, a melodious cracking sound as the Scotch hit the ice cubes, followed by a conditioned response of well-being even before taking a sip.

As he was relaxing in his study, sipping his Scotch and opening the mail, the telephone rang. The caller I.D. indicated that it was a New York City call.

"Garth, this is Julia."

"I was just thinking about you." It was a truthful statement.

"I wasn't sure if you had my number. It's in your call log on your cell phone, but then I realized that you might have received several other area code 212 calls this weekend. So, I called. I hope that's alright. You're not having company?"

"No. I'm glad you called. Actually, I have your number on the playing card you gave me. I am just sitting here by myself going through the mail. How is your grandmother?"

"She's doing quite well. She's been having these fainting spells lately, and the doctors really can't trace them to a specific cause. It's worrisome, but actually, I just think it's her age. It's amazing she is still alive, given the way she drinks."

"Jean Lortigue told me she was frequently the life of the party back in the day."

"Garth, she still is. Wait until you see her this Saturday at your dinner. I guarantee she won't faint while a party is going on. Garth, I know I said this a number of times, but I truly had a lovely time being with you this weekend. My grandmother asked about whether I liked you almost immediately when

I saw her in the hospital. If you haven't figured it out, putting us together was her idea. I went along with it to please her, but I insisted on her making an assessment of you at the lunch on Friday before I would agree to meet with you. I know I am going on, but she was incredibly comical. After you left the Waldorf, she called me immediately and said 'It's a definite go.' She even told me that you smelled nice. I was actually anxious about having lunch with you, but as I told you, I am rather good at hiding my fear. And, of course, I did not tell Agnes about our virtual sleepover. You won't tell her, will you?"

Matthews smiled. She was indeed going on, but there was a definite charm about it. Matthews had come to understand with just a few hours to reflect on the weekend, that Julia really was different than other women he had met since his wife died. She was enigmatic, but she knew it, and she was almost transparent about it, if that's possible.

"Julia, I enjoyed our time together immensely. I am truly looking forward to being with you again this coming weekend…"

"Well, that's one of the reasons I called."

"You're not going to be there?"

"Oh yes, yes. I wouldn't miss it. But, there is a possibility I might see you before then. Oh, I know this is going to sound forward, even presumptuous, but I have been planning to come to Chicago to meet with an art history professor at the University of Chicago. We have been working on a project together. Of course, I could just fly in and out in one day and not bother you at all. But this University of Chicago professor, Nancy McGowen, has been invited to the reception for the new Dean of the College of Business at Lortigue University on Tuesday evening. Oh, I am going on again, but you might wonder why she is invited. It's actually because she is acquainted with Frank Karl, the President of Lortigue. They know each other through the Art Museum. They have a mutual appreciation of art and they serve on some committee together. Garth, are you still there?"

"Yes…"

"I know I seem to be rambling, but the reception is at the President's home in River Forest. According to McGowen, the President has some wonderful artwork, including at least one piece by Schoenling that I have been studying.

Now, here is the presumptuous part: Can I go with you? Oh, I know I am going to be anxious about asking you after we hang up, but this would mean a great deal to me."

The request was forward and presumptuous, but it seemed almost natural coming from Julia.

"Actually, I know about the reception, but I hadn't even noticed that it would be held at the President's house."

"Then I take it, I can't go."

"Of course you can. And I would love to see you before this weekend."

"Oh Garth, thank you. Thank you." Her voice had the sincere gratitude of a child.

"I have only been to the President's house a few times, usually for functions like this. Come to think about it, he does have a great deal of artwork on the walls. I just never had the opportunity to appreciate it. I have always been preoccupied with making conversation with someone."

"Garth, I promise I will not be a burden. I will stay at the Peninsula. I will even pick you up. I will leave on Wednesday morning directly from the hotel. This is such a wonderful favor, and honestly, I am not sure if my motivation is that I just want to see you."

Matthews once again found her to be enigmatic, but oddly transparent about it nevertheless.

"Julia. This is not at all a burden. I will be very proud to have you as my date. Now let's make sure I have this right. This will be our second date, isn't it?"

"Yes. Yes. Our second date."

"Can I make reservations for you at the Peninsula?"

"No. I will take care of everything. I will send you an e-mail with all the details. Garth, you haven't unpacked yet, have you?"

"No. Why?"

"Nothing really," now Julia sounded playful.

"Julia, now don't agonize about this after you hang up. I am incredibly glad that you asked for this favor."

"Thank you, Garth, thank you. Good night…"

Matthews looked for his overnight bag which was in the front hall. He opened the luggage and found something Julia had put there through some sleight of hand. There was a small box, gift-wrapped in light blue paper. He opened it. Inside was a tiny Tiffany crystal glass slipper.

CHAPTER SEVEN

MONDAY

MONDAY MORNING MATTHEWS FOLLOWED his ritual of arriving at the office with coffee and a bagel in a bag. He skimmed the New York Times and the Wall Street Journal. When Rose arrived, he asked her to come into the office.

"Rose, you would not believe the weekend I had in New York. It was both strange and wonderful."

"Then I take it you had a good time."

"Yes, I did. But it was all very surprising. You remember Jeanette Cartere? She is not what you would expect when she is in a social setting."

"You mean she wasn't all business?"

"Not at all. In fact she is, well, a heavy drinker, and her personality changes completely when she has some liquor in her."

"No. Really?"

"Yes, really. And this was at lunch. She was giggling and belching through-out the entire meal! Mrs. Schmidhausen turned out to be quite eccentric and funny. She also drinks a bit, but she seems to be able to handle it better than Cartere. She is very sharp for her age, and she had obviously read some research about legal education before our lunch. And then I met Mrs.

Schmidhausen's granddaughter. She is completely different than her grand-mother. She's a professor at Hunter College and quite charming."

"Is she single?"

"Yes, why do you ask?"

"Because you just smiled when you talked about her."

"Rose, you don't miss a thing." He blushed slightly. "And they are chang-ing the date of the dinner again. It will be this Saturday. I will probably leave Thursday evening. What's on my schedule?"

"Nothing we can't rearrange. I'll take care of it."

After Rose left his office, Matthews opened his e-mail. Most of it was routine. There was an e-mail from Christine Knowel reminding him of the dinner plans that evening at her place at 7:00.

The day progressed with Matthews almost totally unaffected by the distraction of the Schmidhausen Award. He was patient with his staff, gra-cious with potential donors at lunch, and kind to the two faculty members who individually met with him about personal problems. He was, perhaps, somewhat more buoyant than usual, but no one seemed to notice, except of course, Rose.

At 6:45 he left the office and took a cab to Christine's condominium which was located on Lake Shore Drive, just north of the Miracle Mile.

He rang the doorbell of her unit on the seventh floor. She opened the door and threw her arms around Matthews in one motion, and given the fact that he had his business case in one hand, he could only reciprocate with a one-arm hug.

"Garth, I am so glad to see you, safe and in one piece." She backed away from him a few feet and said, "Let me look at you..." What she really was say-ing was, 'look at me.' She had on a garment that, for all his years as a single man, he could not exactly identify. It wasn't exactly a dress, and it wasn't exactly lingerie. It appeared to be made of satin. It was off-white in color, and the neckline plunged well below Christine's cleavage to a waist line that was just north of her navel. From the way the material clung around her ample breasts, it was apparent to Matthews that she was not wearing a bra. Her feet were bare.

"Christine, you look lovely. Absolutely lovely."

"Why thank you, Garth. Please hang up your coat and take off your jacket and tie."

Matthews did what he was asked, and Christine led him into the living room. He had not been to her condominium before, and he found her taste in furnishings to be unusual. As he surveyed the room, he saw a very contemporary couch, tables with glass tops, chairs that looked questionably comfortable and industrial motif lamps. He managed to take this all in while glancing covertly at Christine's breasts only once.

"Have a seat, and I'll bring you a Scotch. You might want to check out the view of the lake."

Matthews selected one of the questionably comfortable chairs, mainly to determine whether it really was as it appeared. He was surprised that it was to his liking. Somehow the chair looked more uncomfortable than it actually was. A clever feat of design, thought Matthews.

Christine brought Garth his Scotch, and with her own Scotch in hand, she sat on the couch directly across from Garth.

"Garth, I promised you I would give you a full report on the Schmidhausens. Let's get that out of the way, and then we can relax and have fun for the rest of the evening."

Matthews had never been given a briefing by someone in Christine's attire, but his life had been recently filled with novel experiences.

Christine went into another room and re-emerged with a file of notes.

"Garth, I don't want to alarm you, but I have unearthed a number of very sobering facts about the Schmidhausens. Some of these facts would lead me to believe that you could be in danger." Christine put on her reading glasses which perched on the end of her nose. Somehow, this transformed her appearance completely, and she looked immediately more like a lawyer, a lawyer wearing lingerie, but still a lawyer. "I really don't like to ruin this award for you, but I care about you so much, I just don't want this award to, well, blow up on you."

"I understand. I genuinely appreciate that you are concerned about me."

"Well, here goes:

"First, I think you heard about the last recipient of the award, Mr. Wooleyfin. At first we thought he was dead. We know now that he is not dead, but we are not sure exactly what has happened to him. I know this sounds bizarre, Garth, but we believe he is being held captive by the Schmidhausens. We are not certain how they are accomplishing this, but we think that they have bribed a judge in New York, and through some trumped up charges, Wooleyfin was convicted of a crime and he was sentenced to house arrest. We are still investigating this."

"What possible motive would the Schmidhausens have for holding him captive?"

"We're not sure, but it is possible he knows something that they don't want him to disclose. He wouldn't be a credible source of information if he were under house arrest."

Christine continued, "Second, while their money was made legitimately during most of the Twentieth Century, in fact they actually did heroic things in hiding Jews from the Nazis. They now appear to be engaging in illegal activities."

"What type?"

"The ugliest business is engaging in sexual trafficking of underage women from Viet Nam. They have built in several layers of entities between the procurement and the placement of the women, but it appears that their involvement is in Viet Nam itself."

The thought of this made Matthews' stomach churn, and he took a healthy swallow of his Scotch in the hope it would have a calming effect.

"The other business in which they appear to be involved is counterfeit prescription drugs. This is a global business, and it draws on sources from many countries. Basically, it involves repackaging inferior medications that are produced under much less stringent standards than we apply in the United States. Next time you take your staten medication, think about that."

Matthews didn't take staten medications, but he got the point.

"Finally, they operate banks in several foreign countries. We are not certain what activity they are camouflaging with these banks, but it is clear that they have the ability to loan billions of dollars to foreign governments. By calling in the loans, they can actually create instability in foreign markets. We think that it is quite possible that they are financing terrorist organizations."

All of this sounded quite plausible to Matthews.

"You might wonder how they maintain control of this vast operation? That's a nice question. We know this: The matriarch of the family, Agnes Schmidhausen, is still alive, and she is in her eighties. She lives in New York. It's almost unbelievable, but she still calls the shots. It appears that her late husband, who was from Zurich, had mafia type connections throughout Europe, and as the world economy changed, he transformed the empire to operate more like a confederacy of franchises. They have operatives in every major European city, each of whom has selected his own racket. Much of the Schmidhausen fortune has been systematically reduced to cash, and the money was used to acquire a broad network of banks that finance the operations in the various cities."

"So the operation is headquartered in New York?"

"New York and Zurich."

"Who else is involved in New York?"

"There are actually a large number of bankers and financial experts who work in New York in the financial district. Also, there is a staff that occupies three floors in a midtown office tower that operates in concert with the staff in Zurich. Hans Schmidhausen, Agnes' son, who lives in New York, believes he is running the operation, but he is basically delusional. He is a strange one."

This was sounding all too real to Matthews, and he began to think that his quaint luncheon with Mrs. Schmidhausen and Mrs. Cartere belied the enormity, and possible treachery, of the Schmidhausen operation. He at once felt naïve not to have even thought about the massive machinery that produces vast sums of money for the Schmidhausens, regardless of how the money was used.

"Are Mrs. Schmidhausen and her son the only members of the family who lives in New York?" Matthews did not want to ask directly about Julia.

"No. There is Schmidhausen's son, and we believe, her granddaughter."

"You're uncertain about her granddaughter?"

"Yes. She appears to have kept a very low profile in the operation for years. She spent her early years in Paris, but has lived in the states since college. There may have been some estrangement at some point with her grandmother, or the family may have kept her insulated from the ugly part of their operations. But she is fully involved now, and she appears recently to have become very close to Mrs. Schmidhausen. In fact she could be the most duplicitous and dangerous member of the family."

"Dangerous?"

"Yes, she's probably the smartest member of the family. In fact her academic credentials are remarkable. But she has been able to keep much of her life concealed from any scrutiny. She makes regular trips to Europe, totally alone, and she was once involved with a very unsavory character who is now doing time at Ithaca. We believe that the two of them may have been involved in some nefarious activity, and they had a falling out. We think the prosecution cut a deal with her to testify against him. Part of the record is sealed, purportedly to protect her privacy."

Matthews was feeling at once deflated and foolish. How could he have let himself get so caught up in a weekend that seemed so innocent and guileless? The part that bothered him most was that, contrary to his sophistication as an accomplished lawyer, he had allowed himself to be oblivious to what had to be a huge global operation that fueled the Schmidhausen fortune.

"Garth, you seem like you are lost in thought."

"I'm sorry. What else do you know about the granddaughter?"

"We think she is very deceptive and cunning. She hangs out with people who claim to be mystics and fortune tellers: very strange people. And we know she has assumed fictitious identities, at least two times in the last five years. She is just very hard to pin down as a person."

"Does she have a career?"

"Right now she is holding herself out as a college professor, but we haven't been able to verify any of it."

"Anything else I need to know?"

"That's what we have so far."

"What do you think I should do?"

"Well, the award is real. I am sure they will deposit your award in your Swiss bank account if you accept it. But if we are right about these people, they would have the ability to remove the funds without a trace, at the very least making you look like a fool in the process. As to the award, I would strongly urge you to decline it and walk away from these people now. There is no other living recipient other than Wooleyfin, and we can't make contact with him. We just know that by giving you this award, you have been targeted in some way. I know that the award may involve a few thousand dollars, but your reputation and your physical safety are much more valuable."

"Thanks, Christine," said Matthews, not correcting Christine about the amount of the cash prize. "Do you really think I am in any physical danger?"

"That is very hard to tell. Clearly, if they have any reason to harm you, they have the capability to do it. But they would have to have a reason. We think that Wooleyfin had them investigated and questioned them about their activities. It would seem that as long as they don't know that you have knowledge about how they operate, you are not in danger. Consequently, you should never reveal anything I am telling you to anyone. The trust that supports the award has been in existence since 1952. It is a legitimate trust, and according to the language in the trust instrument, the terms must be carried out every five years. The award has become much larger than anyone anticipated, and it is conceivable that some members of the family could feel that it is ridiculous to give out such a large award. I guess you could be in danger if someone in the family truly believed that you should not receive an award of this size, but in truth, this is small change to the Schmidhausen family."

"How much do you think the award is?" asked Matthews.

"I really can't even guess. It depends on how the funds in the trust have been invested."

Matthews was impressed with Christine's clear-headed, analytic abilities, and he was grateful for her advice. He felt that she was genuinely concerned about him, and since his wife had died, he had not felt that a woman had been so protective of him. He momentarily felt very safe.

"Garth, let me refresh your drink." She left the room, and Matthews admired her figure as she turned her back to head toward the kitchen. When she returned with fresh drinks for each of them, she still had her reading glasses perched on her nose. She sat down directly across from Matthews, and raised her glass.

"To Garth Matthews. A scholar and a gentleman and a person most deserving of the Schmidhausen Award, but who should nevertheless decline it."

"Cheers," replied Matthews.

Christine smiled and sat back on the couch. She removed her reading glasses and put them on the glass-top cocktail table. She sipped her Scotch, tilted her head back and shook her hair slightly. One of her shoulder straps fell down, and she put it back in place pulling the fabric of the dress tight around her breast. Matthews tried to ignore what was hardly a mishap.

"Christine, what if we found out that there was no danger in accepting the Schmidhausen award. What do you think I should do with the money?" asked Matthews.

"I would take a leave of absence for a few months and travel. Of course, it's no fun traveling alone, so I would take me along," she said with a smile. "Think of the fun we could have. Garth, you really haven't discovered how much fun I can be. I would be a wonderful companion."

Matthews immediately recognized that the statement was sexually encrypted.

"Well, it would be fun to travel. I am sure you would be a wonderful companion."

"I would be the best companion you could ever imagine."

That's not encrypted at all, thought Matthews. He did not know exactly how to respond, and consequently, he changed the subject. "What are we having for dinner?"

"Beef Wellington," was Christine's response.

They walked into the candlelit dining room where the view of Lake Michigan was spectacular. A bottle of CADE '07 Estate Cabernet Sauvignon Howell, was on the table. Matthews knew that virtually any offering from the CADE Winery was considered a serious wine.

"This is a wonderful selection, Christine," said Matthews admiring the label of the bottle. "I have had wine from their sister winery, 'Plumpjack,' but this will be a real treat."

Christine smiled confidently realizing that her wine selection had its intended effect of impressing Matthews.

"I hope it lives up to its reputation. I briefly met one of the CADE wine-makers when I was in Napa. He recommended this wine in particular. He told me it would stand up for a long period of aging, so I bought a case. I bring out a bottle only for special occasions."

Christine had previously uncorked the bottle, and it had been breathing for a while.

"Here, try some." She poured a small amount into his glass. He went through the steps of the ritual: smelling the cork, holding the glass only by the stem, swirling the wine in the bowl, checking the bouquet, and then took a sip.

"Wonderful!" Matthews thought if it tasted like vinegar, he would have said the same thing. But it did not at all taste like vinegar, and it was truly a remarkable full-bodied, dense wine.

Christine could see that he genuinely liked the wine, and she poured him a glass and one for herself.

"I'll take you out to Napa and we can talk to several winemakers. You can sample dozens of wines. Whatever wine you like, you can buy cases and have them sent to Chicago. We can hire a driver, and sample the wine until we are intoxicated. We can do what we please in the back seat as we are driven from one winery to the next."

As they ate dinner, Christine continued to seductively describe the places they should visit together: "London for the theatre; Berlin because of its unique role in Twentieth Century history; St. Petersburg for the art; Rome for the monuments; and Paris for the food." Before Christine had completed her travelogue, Matthews' mind started to drift. He started to analyze Christine's briefing on the Schmidhausens, and he felt that he was quite undecided as to what was the truth. He realized that he did not want to believe Christine, but after reflecting on the matter, he recognized that he had no reason to doubt her, except that his instincts told him that Julia and Agnes seemed incapable of the ugly behavior attributed to them.

Dessert was fruit and gelato, and when Garth declined coffee and said that he had to leave, Christine appeared startled and flustered.

"Garth, we have been getting along so well, I really, you know, expected that you would stay tonight."

This, of course, came as no surprise to Matthews who knew that Christine was creating the predicate for that outcome all evening. How could there be any doubt when she opened the door to her apartment and looked like something most men would consider to be a delivery from the heavens. Moreover, her attempts at sexual encryption in her statements were blatantly transparent. Matthews actually liked Christine, and he did enjoy her company. She was smart, worldly, and sometimes witty. But sleeping with her? No. Not now. Maybe not ever. And at that moment in her apartment, he was not sure he could say why. He just knew that he did not want to spend the night with her.

"Have I done something wrong?" asked Christine, sounding wounded.

"Not at all. I have had a lovely evening. I just don't feel that the time is right." It was a simple, truthful statement.

"I have Viagra…" said Christine, now sounding a little desperate.

"No. That's not it." He gave her a hug, grabbed his coat, jacket, tie and business case from the hall closet and left.

As he rode in the cab back to his house, he started to think about Christine's briefing. He pulled a pad out of his business case and started to make notes about what he had been told:

Trafficking in underage women

Counterfeit drugs

Corrupt use of banking and financial markets

Julia: cunning and dangerous

The cab let him off at his house, and Garth opened the door and went straight to his study. He turned on his computer, and googled Hunter College. He used the "find" screen to type in "Julia Nghiem." He had not done this before on his own computer. He had only seen Julia's credentials on her I-Phone. He felt somewhat anxious for reasons that were not entirely clear to him.

The screen popped up: 'Julia Nghiem, Professor of Art History,' just as it had on Julia's I-Phone. Her picture was there as well, and Matthews just stared at it for a few moments.

He opened his e-mail and clicked on a message from Julia.

"I am arriving early tomorrow morning and spending the day at the University of Chicago. I will pick you up at your house at 6:30. Depending on traffic, we should be at the President's house between 7:00 and 7:30. Please wear your blue blazer. It is very becoming. I think it is best for now if you simply introduce me to people as Julia Nghiem. I don't think we should reveal the Schmidhausen connection yet. I am so glad I will be with you... I have missed you."

Matthews wrote back:

"I have missed you too."

CHAPTER EIGHT

TUESDAY

TUESDAY MORNING, ONE WEEK since he had learned of the Schmidhausen Award, Matthews arrived at his office right on schedule with coffee and a bagel in a bag. He skimmed his newspapers, ate his bagel and turned on his computer promptly at 9:00.

He noticed that he had an e-mail from Jean Lortigue: "Georges and I are both coming to Chicago for the reception for the Dean of the College of Business. If it would not be an imposition, we wonder if you would clear your schedule to have lunch with us. Can we meet in the lobby of the University Club at noon?"

Without checking his schedule, Matthews wrote back that he could.

"Rose," Matthews pushed his chair backwards with his legs until he could make eye contact with her through the door. "What do I have on the schedule for lunch today? The Lortigues would like to have lunch with me."

"The Lortigues? Of course. Nothing we can't rearrange. Let me look. You have lunch scheduled with Professor Williston. Let's see, we can reschedule him for next week. When he scheduled the lunch he said he just wanted to catch up on a few things. I don't think it was anything urgent."

"Tell him that if there is anything he needs right away, I can meet with him this afternoon."

Matthews always tried to be sensitive to the needs of his faculty, and he knew that the slightest, most innocent action or statement could be taken as a snub if not handled properly. Rose understood that as well, and she would handle Professor Williston with consummate diplomacy.

At 11:45, Matthews left for the University Club which is within walking distance from the College of Law. The Club, which has been in existence since 1887, is a private institution unaffiliated with any particular university. It had moved into its current facilities in the first decade of the Twentieth Century. At the time of its completion in 1909, with twelve stories, it was the tallest gothic skyscraper in the world. It housed a dining hall, Cathedral Hall, that was a replica of Crasky Hall built in 1470 in Bishopsgate in the district of London called at that time "the city." The room is considered one of the most beautiful dining rooms in Chicago, with stained glass windows and gothic detail throughout. The Lortigues were members, as was Matthews, and Georges and Jean would always stay at the Club in the guest rooms when they were in Chicago.

Matthews waited for the Lortigues in the lobby of the Club. They had checked in earlier, and they made their entrance from the elevators. Georges and Jean were only about two years apart in age, and when they both had full beards, they looked like twins. Today they were each clean-shaven, and while neither could be called fat, they certainly weren't trim. They had a robust, burley healthiness that reflected a lavish life style.

Matthews rushed to the elevator to greet Georges and Jean, and received a manly hug from each of them.

Matthews genuinely loved these men and tears came to his eyes because he hadn't seen either in two or three months. When Georges and Jean saw the tears well up in Matthews' eyes, they each started weeping as well. They were all dabbing their eyes with handkerchiefs as they boarded the elevator car to go to the Cathedral Room, and when the door closed, they laughed robustly at their own behavior.

As they entered the room, the hostess greeted them each by name, "I have reserved a table in the alcove for you." The alcove, as it is called, houses the most intimate tables in the room. It has a magnificent view of Lake Michigan like the rest of the room, but it was a relatively small, intimate space when compared with the voluminous size of the remainder of the Cathedral Room. It also had a working fireplace which made the space even more inviting. Interestingly, the alcove was the conception of the architect, Martin Roche, and there wasn't a counterpart in Crasky Hall after which the Cathedral Room was modeled.

After they were seated, they each went through the litany of questions inquiring about health, heart, and happiness. For some people this exchange of information would be a matter of empty ritual. But these men truly cared about one another, and the questions were sincere. After it was established that each of them was well, Georges revealed he was in love with a Swiss woman by the name of Gerta, and that he thought he would propose marriage to her during the summer. They raised their water glasses in a toast. Jean explained that he was trying to honorably date two women, one in Paris and the other in London. He acknowledged that he was getting too old for this sort of thing, and that he would have to make a choice before it destroyed his health. He explained that he fancied the woman in London the most, but that he liked the city of Paris more than London. They raised their water glasses in a toast to Jean and expressed sympathy for his dilemma.

It was Matthews' turn.

"I am not really in a serious relationship with anyone, but I have two women who appear to be interested in me. Busy as I am, that's pretty good."

"Are you in love with either of them or both of them?" asked Jean.

"Actually, it is too early to tell."

"Jean, our boy is too shy to tell the truth. I think he is in love with one of them," said Georges, and they all laughed.

They all knew the menu quite well, and they ordered lunch.

"Well Garth," said Georges, "It is great to see you in such fine form. And the Schmidhausen Award is marvelous, and we are delighted that you have been selected. We know that the cash award has become quite large, although we certainly don't know the amount. Frankly, we don't care to know, but we will be letting you pick up the check for dinner from time to time."

They all laughed.

"I'll be glad to," said Matthews.

Georges continued, "We have looked into the questions you have raised about the Schmidhausens. The last thing we would want is for you to be embarrassed by this award."

Matthews felt a tension run through his body.

"We have contacts in every major city in Europe, the Mid East and Northern Africa. These are people who would know if the Schmidhausens were involved in questionable activities. This is what we found. The Schmidhausens are detested by the Neo Nazi movement in Europe, especially in Germany, and more specifically in Berlin. They have been subject to a smear campaign, particularly in Germany. But Garth, these detractors are Neo Nazis, and it is not surprising that they detest the Schmidhausens. During the Second World War, that family hid more Jews from the Nazis than any other network. It was when the Schmidhausens started using their own name again that these hate groups started attacking them. And, of course, the Schmidhausen money now is largely in banking. They have great financial power throughout Europe, and as you might expect, they are very careful as to whom they loan their money. And, of course, they are not apolitical as to how they use their massive fortune, but there is nothing corrupt about what they are doing. For example, they have loaned massive amounts of money to interests in the United States and Britain. Russia? Nothing. It's their choice; it is a private bank."

Matthews breathed a quiet sigh of relief. He could trust the Lortigues.

"And what about the family in New York?" asked Matthews, trying not to show a special interest in Julia.

"As you well know, Agnes is still alive, much to our delight. She is a charming lady, as I am sure you had discovered. There is also Agnes' son who gives the appearance that he manages the operation. Actually, he is something of an odd duck, and Agnes would never give him control over the Schmidhausen Foundation. He is your age, I would say. He shuttles between New York and Zurich, but he really doesn't make any strategic decisions."

"And the granddaughter?"

"Yes, the granddaughter. She is something of an enigma. As far as we can tell, she grew up in Paris and has maintained her distance from the operation and the rest of the family. She appears to be in her own world, and it seems her parents were as well. This happens in some well-to-do families. Some members just don't want to be near the center of wealth. They just don't feel comfortable with it."

Matthews sighed quietly in relief a second time.

"But here is our concern with the granddaughter: She has assumed different identities over the past five years, which of course, makes no sense. We can think of no reason for it."

"Does Agnes know this?" Matthews asked.

"We have no way of knowing. The granddaughter just seems to have her own agenda. She is very smart, and she is probably the most educated of her whole family. Maybe that's why she has maintained distance from the rest of the family until recently. Lately, she seems to have become closer to Agnes. Perhaps she is one of those people who cares little about money and more about her career. But let me say this, if there is one person in that family around whom you should watch yourself, it is the granddaughter. She just seems out of step with the rest of the family."

Swell, thought Matthews.

Their lunches were served.

"Garth," said Jean, "there is another matter we want to discuss with you."

"Yes, of course."

Jean continued, "How do you feel about Frank Karl?"

"The University President? Well, I don't have strong feelings about him, but it is clear that he dislikes me. He always seems so damn uncomfortable around me. There is one thing I like about him, however, that has made any of my other concerns diminish in importance. He lets me run the College of Law. In that respect he is an ideal President. Occasionally, he asks me to do ridiculous things, but when I refuse, he becomes very agitated and critical. But he seems to get over it. Why do you ask?"

"We haven't discussed this with anyone except a few trustees in whom we have confidence. Frank Karl is going to be relieved of the Presidency."

"Well that comes as a surprise," said Matthews, but in some sense it did not.

"We thought you should know, because he may have received some hint about this. But he has been told nothing. Certainly other deans have no idea, and we doubt if anyone really anticipates that he is going to be removed."

"Can you share with me what is behind this?" asked Matthews.

"Yes, we are glad to. But keep in mind that no one else in the administration has this information. Basically, he has been a disappointment, and he has not matched his predecessor, Andrew McAndrews, in vision or competence. Andy was a real leader, and his drive was remarkable. It is a shame that Andy had to retire, but the stress was too much for him. After his third heart attack, we told him that we couldn't bear to think that the position had killed him. How's your heart, Garth?"

"Oh, fine."

"Good. Well, here's the main problem with Karl. He has done wonders with the endowment. He is very close to the Finance Committee of the Board of Trustees. But he acts like that is the full responsibility of the job. The endowment has grown magnificently, mainly through creative investments by the Finance Committee, but that is really not the President's doing. It would be one thing if he was a successful fundraiser, but he really hasn't raised that much money through philanthropy. It's all been the Finance Committee's work. In any event, Karl gets failing grades in every other aspect of the job."

"I have noticed that the increase in the endowment is remarkable," offered Matthews.

"The President's job is to drive the success of the University not just financially, but also in terms of academic stature. The President of Lortigue needs vision to understand how the University can become the peer of the University of Chicago and Northwestern. You were recruited by Andy who understood that the way to have a great university is to have great colleges headed by extraordinary deans, deans that can recruit talented faculty from highly regarded universities. Frankly, the College of Law is the only college that is excelling. Karl has appointed mediocre people with whom he is comfortable. He is clearly not comfortable with you because the reputation of the Law School far exceeds that of the University."

Matthews was deeply appreciative of what Jean was telling him. For the most part, Matthews was able to ignore the rest of the University in the management of the College of Law, which was something any law school dean could do. Unlike the other colleges, which are linked together by a common budget, a law school operates independently with its own budget, its own admissions staff, its own library and its own distinct faculty.

"Garth, here is what we need you to think about," said Jean in a whisper. "We don't know exactly when Karl will be removed, but we want to make it graceful for him and for the University. But when it happens, we will need someone to step in as the Interim President. Garth, you undoubtedly know where this is going…"

He did.

He never had the ambition of being a University President. And stepping away from the deanship of the College of Law might mean that the law school would regress. It would be very painful for Matthews to see the law school falter in any way. But he also understood that Jean was painting an accurate picture about the leadership of the University, and he knew that there are times in life when a person has to put loyalty first. The Lortigues were his best friends, and he knew he could not turn them down.

"Yes, I do know where this is going. But I want you to know that I have never had aspirations of being a university president. I have been truly happy as dean of the law school. That is really where my commitment lies."

"Well, we will take this one step at a time," said Jean "You don't know - you might like being President. But if you don't, at least this is one way you can find out. We are only asking that you be ready to step in as Interim President."

"I owe it to both of you. I can't turn you down."

"Of course. We knew that's what you would say. After all, we know you like new adventures."

Tuesday afternoon at 4:00, Matthews told Rose he was leaving early because he would be attending the reception at President Karl's home.

At his house, Matthews took a shower and selected his wardrobe for the reception: gray slacks, a white shirt, a striped tie and the new navy blazer that Julia had asked him to wear.

Promptly at 6:30, Matthews' doorbell rang, and as he approached the door, he could see Julia's silhouette through the stained glass. Despite all the apprehension created by the report from Christine, Matthews was definitely eager to see Julia. Even if he was being deceived, he was intrigued by the illusion. He opened the door, and she immediately hugged him.

"I am so glad to see you," she whispered, although there was no one around who might have heard her had she used a normal tone of voice. "It seems like forever since I last saw you."

Julia had on a long black designer dress. Her earrings and necklace were diamonds, and her hair was long and loose.

"Garth, you wore the navy blazer, just as I asked. You look very handsome."

"Thank you. You look lovely, and I will be very proud to be with you. Well, I am ready. Shall we leave to fight the Chicago traffic?"

"Yes, the car is double-parked."

As they walked to the white Lincoln Town Car, the driver sprung out of the car and opened the back door. Julia entered the back seat, and slid over to the far side of the seat. Matthews took his seat. The driver had the GPS device set for President Karl's residence in River Forest, and they were on their way.

Julia and Garth each put on a seat belt, and consequently, from the positions at either side of the car, they were able to turn and face one another.

"Well, Garth, how are you adjusting to the idea of becoming one of the greatest and wealthiest leaders in the free world?"

"So far, it does not appear to have had any effect whatsoever. I have thought about it. How could I not? I've thought about buying a vintage Jaguar roadster, but I had thought about that before I learned of the award. And I did buy this blue blazer, but that wasn't really an extravagance."

"You mean you bought that in New York?"

"Yes. Actually, because you suggested it."

"I did? Oh, I guess I did."

"I have thought about traveling to some exotic locations but I really can't be away from the deanship for long periods of time. Do you like to travel?"

"Actually I do, but I really haven't had someone to accompany me, so I usually travel alone. That can take the fun out of it. When I was a child, my family traveled a great deal."

"Would you like to join me sometime, perhaps after we get to know each other a little better? We could have virtual sleepovers on a trip."

Julia laughed. "I would never impose myself on you as a travel partner, but if it is something you would want to do, I could be packed tomorrow. Actually, I would have to finish teaching my courses this semester, but I would love to travel with you."

Matthews kept reminding himself that he had known Julia for less than a week, and he didn't want to make any vacant promises. He also felt compelled not to discount the warnings he had received from Christine, despite the reassurances he received about the Schmidhausen family from the Lortigues.

"Julia, let's consider the possibility of going on a trip after your classes are over and I have graduation behind me. Graduation ceremonies are a command performance for deans."

"Oh Garth! Really? You would consider that? Just your consideration of it makes me incredibly happy." Her face reflected a childlike excitement that was in no way incongruent with her elegance.

Matthews momentarily studied her expression, and he asked himself, could this possibly be the face of a person who engaged in monstrous international criminal activities? He tried not to let his own face betray his thoughts. He found the idea of Julia engaging in anything so dreadful to be unimaginable, and his facial expression did not change at all.

"Garth, tell me about the President. Do you know him well?"

"Actually, I don't. He lets me run the law school without interference, which is what I like about him. He is primarily concerned with the undergraduate colleges. Most of the University meetings I attend with him have little or nothing to do with the law school. We don't see each other socially except on occasions like this. I have only been to his house a few times, and he is usually very pleasant when he is at a function like this one."

"His house is in River Forest; how far is that from the city?"

"It's about ten miles due west of the loop. Depending on traffic, it can take less than 25 minutes to get there. The President has an easy commute, particularly since he has a driver. The house itself is an impressive Georgian mansion on the north side of River Forest, near the Dominican University. Lortigue University actually owns the house."

Matthews wanted to tell Julia that Frank Karl's tenure as President was about to reach its denouement, but of course, he did not.

As Julia and Matthews sat quietly for a moment, Matthews started to reflect on his conversation with the Lortigues, regarding assuming the position of Interim President. He really had no apprehension about his ability to manage the responsibilities of the position. In fact, he often felt it was an easier post than that of the dean of the law school, in part because the President has a much larger staff who attend to numerous responsibilities that a law school dean is required to handle himself or herself. For this same reason, however, Matthews was not certain that he would find the position satisfying. The President could easily become the creation of his staff or a small group of powerful trustees, and in the process, lose his or her own sense of direction. Matthews quickly recognized a strong similarity of both wealth and power. With the sudden acquisition of each, or both, one could lose direction. It could happen to anyone.

Matthews looked at Julia, and they smiled at one another. Matthews realized that he was strongly attracted to Julia, and also realized that if it turned out that she had engaged in the ugly behavior which Christine had attributed to her, Matthews' confidence in his ability to accurately judge people would suffer immeasurable damage. He fully appreciated the vulnerable position he occupied, and he reminded himself that he had to maintain his balance. But as adventures go, he thought, this was really a good one.

The driver had exited the Eisenhower Expressway and traveled north on Harlem Avenue. He then turned left to enter River Forest, as the GPS device directed him to President Karl's house. The car pulled up to the door on the circular driveway.

The President's house was a Georgian mansion, probably built in the mid 1920's. It was a house that looked as if it had never been neglected, and prior to its acquisition by the University, it was purportedly owned by a succession of underworld figures, each of whom gave up possession by virtue of his demise at the hands of rival family members. The legend of the house was likely true. River Forest was commonly known to be the neighborhood of choice for Chicago's infamous criminal elite in the twenties and thirties.

As Matthews exited the car and looked up at the imposing structure, he thought that living here would be a nice perquisite of the Interim Presidency. He was quickly distracted from the thought, however, by the sight of Julia gliding out of the seat of the car with aristocratic grace. She appeared even more beautiful than Matthews had remembered, if that were possible. He took her hand as they walked to the door. The evening was unseasonably warm, and the double front doors were standing open, and they made their entrance, arm in arm, without being greeted.

While there was nothing ruggedly handsome about him, Matthews was blessed with refined, intelligent good looks. He was told more than once that he looked like the law school dean from central casting. Accompanied by Julia, their entrance turned heads. Together they looked like they were created by Hollywood, not Harvard and Yale. As they walked through the crowd of guests, people actually stopped talking and stared at them. Matthews knew that they were really looking at Julia, and while he was correct, he played his part admirably in providing a balanced image that the guests obviously found to be striking. As Matthews introduced Julia to people he knew, there was a confidence in the harmony of their movements that represented a significant progression from their first party at Posse's home in New York.

Matthews spotted the President, who was standing near the string quartet. Odd, thought Matthews, that would be the last place he would position himself if he were President. Why would Karl place himself where conversation would be difficult so close to the music? Karl saw Matthews, and a frown immediately came across Karl's face. Crap, thought Matthews, Karl knows

I am going to replace him. Matthews immediately felt sympathy for Karl, imagining how difficult it would be to be asked to step down.

Karl signaled to Matthews that he wished to speak with him. Matthews escorted Julia to where the President stood.

"President Karl, let me present Julia Nghiem. Julia is a professor at Hunter College in New York."

"Professor of what?" said Karl, in a tone bordering on rudeness.

"I am a Professor of Art History. I hear you are a history scholar. Early Eighteenth Century English History, if I recall correctly." Julia could not be more poised.

"Well, it's nice to meet you; I hope you enjoy the art that I have. I have personally collected it." Karl then signaled to Matthews that he would like to speak with him privately. Matthews dreaded the moment. Karl could be suppressing enormous rage if he had learned that his time as President was reaching its end and that Matthews was in any way involved with his termination.

"Matthews, who is this woman?"

Matthews was taken totally by surprise. In fact, he did not know how to react.

"I met Julia on a recent trip to New York. Why do you ask?"

"Well, no reason."

At once Matthews was relieved that the imminent conclusion of Karl's presidency was not the reason for his frown, and at the same time, he felt a sense of outrage at the idea that the President had any concern whatsoever with his personal life. He felt that the most sensible strategy was to disengage from the conversation with Karl immediately. He took Julia by the hand and walked away.

"What was that about?" asked Julia.

"Julia, I wish I knew, because I truthfully do not. I can only tell you that he is no one that you need to be concerned about." He stopped dead there, with no comment about the President's termination. "Let's find some food. I am actually rather hungry."

The buffet was served outdoors, and several doors were open from the back of the house to a beautiful slate patio surrounded by tall trees, many of which were just beginning to bud. As they made their way to the line, Matthews was proud to introduce Julia to several of his colleagues, including the Dean of Arts and Sciences, Gordon Howell, and the Dean of Engineering, Mary Ann Segal.

As they were waiting in line with plates in hand, Matthews asked Julia if she had seen the paintings that had interested her.

"Yes, I have briefly glanced at some on the walls of the living room, but I haven't seen the Schoenling and some other works he is known to have. My friend, Nancy McGowan, the Professor at the University of Chicago with whom I met today, knows the President's collection quite well. When we see her, she will be able to show us the important paintings."

Matthews and Julia dined holding the buffet plates while standing. They were joined by Andy McAndrews, the first President of Lortigue University, and by Georges and Jean Lortigue. After the proper introductions, they talked about the early days of the University and the subsequent founding of the College of Law. Jean and Georges regaled the group with stories about the several times in the first few years of the university's existence when Lortigue almost closed its doors. As the stories were told, it appeared that McAndrews was frequently the person who took some heroic action and pulled Lortigue back from the brink. McAndrews was appropriately modest, and he pointed out the role of other people, including Matthews, in rescuing the University.

Georges tactfully pulled Matthews aside for a moment and whispered in his ear, "This is the one you love. I can tell."

They both looked at Julia who smiled back at them. The setting sun illuminated her face, creating an incandescent image of incredible beauty.

"She is a stunning woman," said Georges. "You two could be very happy in this house," he added with a facetiously tempting tone in his voice.

"Karl has been acting strangely tonight," Matthews whispered to Georges. "Does he know anything?"

"He knows nothing yet. But at some level he understands that he is a failure, and that all his job security is pinned precariously to the Finance Committee. Lots of people are starting to whisper that it is time for him to go."

At that moment Nancy McGowan, the University of Chicago Professor, approached the group, and Julia introduced her to the assemblage.

"Nancy is a brilliant Art History Professor, and we share an interest in certain Old Master painters."

The conversation turned to art, with McGowan and Julia leading the way. Anything Matthews contributed he had learned from Julia, but Jean and Georges had a remarkable knowledge of art, and the conversation became quite animated. As the conversation concluded, McGowan, Julia and Matthews walked as a group to admire the paintings in the living room. McGowan explained the valuable pieces were only brought out of storage and hung for social events. Other paintings of lesser importance held their places on an everyday basis.

After they spent time appreciating each piece, McGowan asked Julia and Matthews to follow her to the hall in the south wing of the mansion. She removed a key from her purse and opened a locked door behind which was an elevator. The three entered the car of the elevator and McGowan locked the outer door before she entered in a code on a panel with a keypad.

"We are going down two levels to a sub-basement that President Karl has used to house his art collection. The paintings on the walls in the living room are stored here when there isn't a social event. He also has a number of other interesting pieces here."

When the elevator car stopped and the door opened, McGowan told Julia and Matthews, "There is no code needed to activate the elevator from this level. Use this button with the '1' on it to return to the hall where we entered the elevator. I am going to rejoin the party. The President is expecting me."

Matthews wasn't entirely sure if this was an authorized visit to the storage area, and he was not going to ask Julia until after McGowan left.

"Julia, does our host know we are down here?"

"I am not sure. But McGowan is the de facto curator of the collection, and she certainly has the authority to show us the gallery."

"I hope you're right," said Matthews, realizing that he didn't need anything else right now that might antagonize the President.

As they walked into the storage gallery, Matthews noticed at once that it was quite different from Posse's gallery. Rather than narrow halls that were obviously designed to create the maximum wall space, Karl's paintings were hung in large rooms which provided a variety of vantage points to view the paintings.

"Oh Garth, here is the Schoenling I wanted to see. Thank you for bringing me. I am so grateful." She took advantage of the large room in which it hung and moved to view the painting from numerous angles and distances. Matthews watched how enthralled she was by the simple viewing of a painting, and he realized that she embraced this opportunity like a gift to be cherished. After she was leaving the room, she hugged Matthews and thanked him again.

Matthews and Julia spent the next hour viewing other artwork. Julia took the time to explain each painting, and Matthews was grateful to add to his rather meager knowledge of art. In one room there were pieces of sculpture. In each case, Julia could identify the period, but not always the sculptor. In another room, presumably the architectural room, there were pieces of furniture from stark contemporary pieces, to antiques from the Seventeenth and Eighteenth Centuries. As they were walking into a room whose walls were covered with exotic rugs and carpets, the lights suddenly went out. There was complete darkness, but shortly, battery powered emergency lights flickered on.

"What do you think happened?" asked Matthews. The question was rhetorical.

"I don't know. Let me call Nancy. She might know," Julia pulled her I-Phone out of her purse, but it was difficult to obtain a signal.

"Let's walk to the periphery of the building; we may be able to get a signal there. Of course, this place is like a labyrinth. Without any natural light, it's hard to figure out where the outer walls are."

"Let's just walk around, and I will look to see if I get a signal."

After several minutes of wandering from room to room, Julia was able to locate a spot that seemed to have a signal. She keyed in McGowan's number. It rang, but shortly the sound stopped. Patiently, Julia tried again.

"Barbara? Thank goodness. What's going on?" She put her I-Phone on the speaker setting.

"There has been a storm. The power grid out here is very temperamental, and the electricity is out. Of course, the house has a generator, but it is connected only to certain key areas. Don't worry, the ventilation for the gallery is operating. You're not going to suffocate."

"I really wasn't worried about that."

"Julia, the gallery was built in a rather clandestine manner. Karl really didn't want too many people to know about it. There was never a building permit, and consequently, there isn't a fire exit. Here is an interesting fact - that space was used to hide gin during prohibition."

Swell, thought Matthews, just what we need now - a history lesson.

Julia interrupted her, "Well, what's the plan. How do we get out?"

"Karl doesn't know you're down there, and while he gets over these things, he might think I abused my power in taking you to the gallery. The guests are leaving, and he and I are going to the bar at Hemingway's in Oak Park to wind down from the party. When the power comes on, just let yourself out. If the security system is set off, don't panic. Just calmly walk away from the house. You will be long gone before the River Forest Police arrive."

Garth spoke up, "Are the River Forest Police slow to react?"

"No Dean, they are very fast to react," replied McGowan, "But the system is designed to protect against people from breaking in, not breaking out."

They all laughed.

"Okay, Barbara. I think we can live with that plan." Julia turned off her I-Phone. "Garth let's find the room with the furniture."

Matthews was slightly upset, not with Julia, but with McGowan. As a lawyer he knew he had done nothing wrong in relying upon her in gaining access to the gallery. But Matthews just did not need any more tension with the President at the moment.

When they found the architectural room, they sat down together on a Queen Anne couch.

"Garth, I hope you can forgive me for this. This is all my fault."

"No. No, it isn't. You had no idea this would happen. But I am not entirely happy with your friend, Barbara McGowan."

"Could you get into hot water over this?"

"No. Just some minor embarrassment."

"Garth, I had no idea that McGowan was overstepping her bounds. Please, please don't hold this against me."

"None of this is your fault. Besides, watching you enjoy the Schoenling and the other pieces made it all worthwhile. That's what really matters."

"Garth, you are the sweetest man. I have been so lucky to meet you."

She took off her shoes, got up, and turned toward Matthews kneeling on the couch next to him. She put her arms around the back of his neck and said, "I am going to kiss you now." And she did, first with a gentle brush of her lips, and then with an intensity that Matthews did not really expect. He put his arms around her, and they continued to kiss until Julia pulled her head back slightly to look at his face. She wanted him to see her smile and to see how happy the kiss had made her. He opened his eyes, and in the dim illumination from the security lights, he just looked at her and returned the smile. Matthews thought he had never really looked at another person's face this closely. He could see each of Julia's eyelashes. The variegated coloring of each of her irises looked like polished river stones, and he marveled at the perfect symmetry of her face. But what he found most intriguing was the way the pigment of her lips created a perfectly defined boundary with the skin on her face, with each having its own distinct beauty. Their foreheads touched slightly, and they continued to look at one another and smile. And then they hugged each other intensely. Although he dared not say it, Matthews knew he was falling in love, and he tried to forget that falling in love with Julia could be the biggest blunder of his life.

As they continued their embrace, the lights flickered and the electricity returned.

"Let's just ignore it," said Matthews, but he knew the light changed the moment.

Julia smiled broadly, and stood up. Matthews took her hand and they found their way to the elevator. As McGowan had explained, there was no code needed to operate the elevator from this level. But when the elevator door opened, they found that the outer door was locked.

"Now what?" said Matthews.

"I'll call Barbara." Julia reached her immediately. Within minutes the bolt of the lock moved, and the door opened. A man, who had just unbolted the door, was standing in the hallway. Matthews could have sworn it was Art Nelson, the man in the blue suit and yellow paisley tie who sat next to him on the flights between Chicago and New York. But he could not be sure, and the man who opened the door just nodded and walked away.

Julia and Matthews walked through the house, and as they passed through the living room, the catering staff was cleaning up after the party.

"We were just using one of the bedrooms," said Matthews as they walked out the front door.

A member of the staff just waved as if it happened all the time.

Julia had called for the car, and it was waiting for them at the front door in the circular driveway.

Julia fell asleep on Matthews shoulder on the way to his house, and barely awoke when the car dropped him off. He kissed her softly on the cheek, and Julia immediately fell back to sleep.

CHAPTER NINE

WEDNESDAY

W EDNESDAY MORNING, MATTHEWS ARRIVED at his office still thinking about President Karl's reception. Rather than read his newspapers, he tried to put together the sequence of events that conspired to create one of the most unusual evenings of his life. He felt he was falling in love with Julia, but this could be a disastrous mistake; he was locked in a secret art gallery where he kissed Julia; he had the opportunity to reconnoiter a mansion that would likely be his next residence; he saw a man who might have been Art Nelson; and President Karl acted rudely and asked him about his personal life. A most unusual evening, thought Matthews, as he finished eating his bagel.

He turned on his computer and scanned the messages.

A message from Jean Lortigue indicated he and Georges were both leaving Chicago on early morning flights. They regretted that they were unable to say goodbye in person. The e-mail expressed appreciation that Matthews was willing to "step up," but it did not expressly mention the Interim Presidency.

An e-mail from Andy McAndrews, the former University President, stated that he was pleased to see Matthews again and that he remembered fondly working with him. He ventured to say that one of the best things he did during his presidency was to appoint Matthews as Dean of the College of Law.

118

Julia sent an e-mail from her I-Phone that said she was about to board her flight back to New York. The message continued, "Garth, I had the most wonderful time being with you. I will never forget the evening. I cannot wait to see you again."

There was an e-mail from Barbara McGowan apologizing for the mishap involving the gallery at the President's residence.

In addition to several other e-mails concerning the operation of the law schools, there was an e-mail from Christine Knowel.

Garth,

I guess I have greatly misjudged our relationship. When you didn't stay Monday evening, I was surprised, but I still had hope that our relationship would continue. When you didn't ask me to join you for the reception at the President's house, I thought you were just busy and intended to make a quick appearance and leave. But when I learned you escorted another woman to the reception, I was crestfallen. I never imagined that there was another woman in your life.

Christine

Matthews immediately felt horrible. While he was curious as to how Christine knew he had escorted Julia to the reception, he really didn't want to hurt Christine in any way. He replied as honestly as he could.

Dear Christine,

I am genuinely sorry that you feel confused and injured. It was never my intention to do anything hurtful. My own life appears to be in a state of transition, and I am honestly somewhat confused myself about my emotions. Nothing that I have done should be perceived by you as rejection. As my life returns to some degree of normalcy, perhaps we can see each other.

Fondly,

Garth

At nine o'clock, Rose arrived. After a few minutes she came into Matthews' office. Rose put some mail on Matthews' desk and said, "I received an e-mail from Bea White, Karl's assistant. The President would like to see you at ten o'clock in his office."

"Of course," said Matthews.

He had not yet mentioned to Rose that the President was soon to be fired. "Rose, come in and close the door... I have been meaning to tell you this, but yesterday was something of a blur. Here's the news: I learned during lunch with the Lortigues that President Karl will be asked to step down in the near future."

"Interesting" replied Rose, "I could have guessed that. But the timing was always a question for me."

"Well, I really don't know what the timing will be. But here is the part that concerns you and me: The Lortigues asked me to step in as the Interim President when the time comes. I really am not interested in becoming the permanent President, but I told Georges and Jean that I could not turn them down. I would only serve until a permanent president is appointed."

"Garth, you would be a wonderful President. You should seriously consider it. We haven't had decent university leadership around here since McAndrews retired."

"That's exactly what Georges and Jean said. Well, there is nothing to be gained in thinking about it now. The time will come soon enough when I am in the Interim President position, and I am sure I will figure out quickly if it suits me or not."

As was his custom, Matthews arrived early for his meeting with President Karl. He really couldn't guess what the President wanted to discuss with him, but he had a foreboding feeling that the conversation would be awkward at best.

"Garth, come in," said Karl. "Sit at the conference table. There is a box of pastries on the table. I think there are some jelly-filled donuts left. Strawberry, the best kind."

Matthews wondered whether Karl had eaten most of the contents of the box. Both men sat down facing one another at the large table. Matthews noticed that the President's moustache, now fairly grown, had several crumbs embedded in the whiskers.

"Garth, first I want to say that I was deeply offended when you did not bother to tell me you were leaving last night. I guess you thought it was permissible to just leave my house without thanking me."

"I am sorry, but...."

"No need to make excuses. I know our relationship has deteriorated completely, and that's why I wanted to speak with you."

Karl reached into the box and removed a jelly donut, inspected it from several angles as if it were a thing of beauty, and stuffed half of it into his mouth. The table was already scattered with donut crumbs of various sizes. Karl continued to talk with his mouth full. Matthews pushed his chair back from the table in fear of being assaulted by bits of pastry projecting from Karl's mouth.

"As you know, Garth, you serve as Dean of the College of Law at the pleasure of the President, and that would, of course, be me. For years I have put up with your insubordination and total unwillingness to be a team player. As President, I need to know that I can count on each and every dean to be on my team. Not the Lortigue brothers' team, but my team. I am afraid I can never be sure that I can count on you. It is for that reason that I am relieving you of the deanship of the College of Law."

From all external appearances, Matthews seemed unshaken. Matthews immediately started to calculate the consequences. If he were removed from the deanship, perhaps, he could not step in as Interim President. Perhaps Karl had learned of the plan to remove him. He wondered if this was some pre-emptive strategy or if Karl simply felt threatened.

"Of course, Frank, if that is your wish. I think before doing this you would want to have the support of the Board of Trustees."

"I have discussed the matter with the Finance Committee, and they are the only trustees that matter."

"Are you sure?"

"You remember the song from Cabaret: 'Money Makes the World Go Round.' What is true for the world is true for the university."

"And when do you want this to occur?" responded Matthews quickly, hoping to preempt the possibility that Karl would start singing.

"I don't want this to hurt the University, and likewise, despite what you may think of me, I don't want this to be awkward for you or damaging to your career. We need to do this in a way that you can easily move on to another

deanship. I suggest that you announce your resignation shortly after graduation, by June first at the latest. You will have a year on the payroll to look for
another position."

"What if I choose not to resign?"

"Oh, you'll be fired summarily and without explanation."

Karl adoringly examined the last morsel of pastry and then popped it in
his mouth.

"I see. Is that all?" asked Matthews, acting like their conversation involved
routine business.

"Well, yes, I guess so," said Karl stuffing the remainder of the jelly donut
in his mouth. "I'll have an agreement drawn up and sent over to you. Here,"
he said pushing the box toward Matthews, "there is one more pastry left."

"No, thank you," said Matthews noticing that some strawberry jam had
oozed out of a donut and landed on the left lapel of Karl's already stained suit.

As Matthews walked back to the law school building, he tried to determine the consequences of the conversation he just had with the President.
He knew he would need to consult Jean and Georges Lortigue as to how
they would want to handle this unanticipated turn of events. He wondered
whether it could possibly be the case that the Finance Committee of the Board
of Trustees could somehow trump the Lortigues' wishes. Unfortunately, he
could not get the song from Cabaret out of his head, but he was relieved that
he did not have to listen to Karl sing it. Karl often sang Broadway show tunes
in his feeble effort to make a point.

When he returned to his office, he asked Rose to come in and close the
door.

"I just had the most remarkable conversation with the President. He fired
me."

"Fired you?"

"Yes, well actually he wants me to resign after graduation, presumably
by June 1."

"Can he do that?"

"I suppose he can, but I assume that Georges and Jean will intercede
and prevent it from happening. In fact, Karl's actions may hasten his own

termination. Here is the intriguing dimension of all this: It would seem to me that if he knew that his own termination is imminent, and if he knew I was designated to step in as Interim President, he would have fired me on the spot. He would have handed me a cardboard carton, told me to clear out my desk, and leave immediately. It's my guess that he doesn't know of the decision to sack him. He is probably concerned about being terminated, but he just doesn't know that it's going to happen in the near future."

"Do you want me to try to reach Jean or Georges?"

"Yes. I don't know where they are at the moment, but see if you can get one of them on the phone."

Rose reached each of the Lortigue assistants, but she learned that both Jean and Georges were on a flight to Paris.

Matthews did his best to concentrate on his work, but his mind kept thinking through the various scenarios that might result from Karl's actions. After realizing that he was too distracted to make serious progress on the matters on his desk, he pushed his chair backward with his feet in order to speak with Rose.

"Do I have any commitments for lunch?"

"No. You are actually free for the rest of the day."

"The weather is pleasant. I think I will take a walk, grab a sandwich somewhere, and try to sort this out."

One hour and twenty minutes later, Matthews returned to his office with a navy blue shopping bag containing a new shirt and tie he had purchased at Brooks Brothers.

He heard Rose's voice as he entered the Dean's suite.

"Garth, come quickly, you have to see this." There was a certain, very unusual urgency in her voice, and he walked briskly to her desk.

Rose turned her computer screen so that Matthews could see the streaming news video. He stared at the screen in stunned silence, as if what he was seeing could not possibly be happening.

After he watched the screen for several minutes, he said, "Rose, when was this first broadcast?"

"I think about ten minutes ago. Bea White, from the President's office, called me."

"This is unbelievable. Just unbelievable"

The streaming video was of an arrest of four men who were entering the Italian Village restaurant, a few blocks from the law school building. The men were President Frank Karl, and the three members of the Board of Trustees Finance Committee.

"Rose, what is this about?"

"I am not entirely sure, because there has been no comment from the police. All we have seen is the video of the arrest. Wait, look, the reporter is putting a microphone in front of the President's face.

"Do you have a comment?" asked the reporter on the video.

"Yes, they could have at least waited to arrest us until after we had lunch," was the President's reply.

The others just tried to hide their faces, appearing to be more embarrassed by the President's statement than the arrest.

Matthews and Rose looked at each other, each with an expression of total amazement.

"I guess we can safely assume that the crime involves money in some way," said Matthews, "And given the cast of characters, it's probably University money."

Rose noticed that the streaming video had changed. It looked like there was about to be a press conference. The F.B.I. logo hung on a blue curtain before which appeared three people.

"Good afternoon" said a male on the video. "I am Assistant United States Attorney, Martin Gainey. To my left is F.B.I. Agent, Robert Murphy and to his left is Special Consultant to the F.B.I. and Special Deputy F.B.I. Agent, Barbara McGowan."

"Oh my God, Rose, I know that woman."

"I trust that you weren't involved with her."

"No. Not involved, not at all. Nothing. Hardly a handshake. Nothing. Honest."

Agent Gainey continued, "Today we arrested four individuals who will be charged with the interstate sale of stolen artwork, the conspiracy to sell stolen art, the possession of stolen artwork, four counts of interstate fraud, and the conspiracy to commit fraud. They are Frank T. Karl, the current President of Lortigue University; Arthur P. Lewis, President of Lorny Investments, Ltd.; Frederick Dorrey, of D.L.P., Inc.; and Patrick L. Crane, Senior Partner at the law firm of Nathan, Barney & North."

Agent Gainey continued, "The individuals standing with me today are members of the Criminal Investigative Division, America's Criminal Enterprise Major Theft Unit. We work under the Art Theft Program Manager in Washington D. C., who heads the Art Crime Team which was established in 2004, partly as a result of the looting of the Baghdad Museum, a matter which required a rapid deployment team to address the immediate problem. Our jurisdiction and operation extends far beyond the problems in Iraq. We currently maintain the National Stolen Art File, and since our inception, we have recovered stolen artwork valued in the millions of dollars. The pieces we have recovered number in the thousands. Nevertheless, art and cultural property crimes are estimated to involve six billion dollars annually. The arrests we made today will lead to charges under Title 18 of the United States Code, Sections 659, 2314, 2315 and most particularly section 668 – Theft of Major Artwork.

"The individuals arrested today have allegedly bought and sold thirty-two pieces of stolen artwork over an eight-year period. As part of their alleged activities, they have fraudulently converted funds from the endowment of Lortigue University, and while the profits from the transactions were in part returned to the endowment, each of the accused individuals has profited substantially. Most, if not all of the currently held stolen artwork we believe is stored at the residence of Mr. Frank, and that residence has been seized by the F.B.I. eighteen minutes ago. We do not believe that anyone else connected with Lortigue University is involved in this matter. We also would like to remind the public that this is an arrest, and every person is presumed innocent until proven guilty. We cannot take any questions at this time. Thank you."

Rose and Matthews turned slowly from the computer screen to look at one another in complete astonishment.

"Well, I guess I don't have to worry about being fired," said Matthews in a subdued tone of voice.

After watching the streaming video of the arrest and the ensuing statements from the F.B.I., Matthews slowly sat down in the chair in front of Rose's desk. "I suspected that something like this would happen," he said, "Just not of this magnitude. I always thought Karl would be capable of being influenced by the wrong kind of people. I am sure that he was not the leader of this little group; he's not clever enough. But this is much larger and more corrupt than I ever imagined."

"Garth, a lot of people suspected there was some type of fraud or embezzlement going on, but certainly not on this scale. I noticed some signs of it when I worked in the Provost's office. Bea White, who works in the President's office, Dorothy Wilhelm who works in the Provost's office, and I have been keeping track of a number of large transactions because they seemed to be suspicious. We've also been getting information from Sue Tyler who works in the Foundation Office."

"Why didn't you tell me about this?"

"Well, to be honest, we weren't sure if it was appropriate to keep this kind of information, and I didn't want to get you involved. Actually, it was sort of a hobby for us to keep track of this stuff. Do you think we did anything wrong?"

"No, I am sure you didn't. But you will have to contact the F.B.I. and the U.S. Attorney's Office and give them this information."

"Of course."

"Do you know how these transactions were described in the University records?"

"Usually, they were purchases of shares of a limited partnership. There were four or five of these partnerships. They just had letters or initials in their names, like 'NTR, LLC.' There would be purchases of, let's say, a hundred shares at a thousand dollars a share. After a year or so, the shares would be sold to another limited partnership for something like two thousand dollars a share. The shares were sold almost always at a considerable gain."

"How could the auditors fail to pick this up?"

"That's a mystery to me, but the Foundation has a different auditor than the University. We just figured they were in on the scheme."

"Were any of the transactions recorded as purchases of artwork?"

"There were some purchases of paintings. And there were substantial purchases for the President's residence, but they were usually listed as 're-decoration' or 'an improvement'."

At this point, people were gathering outside of Rose's office, obviously intent upon gathering information about the President's arrest.

Matthews stepped out into the hall. "I can assure you that I know nothing more than what has been broadcast on the Channel 5 website. This is a total surprise to me. Unless you have some urgent work to finish, please feel free to watch the news. This is a once in a lifetime event."

Matthews returned to Rose's office. "Please send out an e-mail to the faculty and staff that the President's arrest came as a surprise to me and that I only know what is being broadcast on the news channels."

"Just a minute, your direct line is ringing." Rose picked up the phone. "Yes Georges, he will be with you in a moment. It's Georges Lortigue."

"That's strange. I thought he was on a flight to Paris."

Matthews went into his office to take the call.

"Yes Georges. I thought you were on a flight."

"We were at O'Hare ready to board the plane, when we received a call from the U.S. Attorney's office that the arrest was going to occur today. We never boarded the plane."

"So you knew about the President's activities and the investigation?"

"Yes, for some time. The investigation has been going on for quite a while. The F.B.I. figured that the individuals involved would not disappear because they all had prominent positions. The investigative team wanted to collect as much evidence as possible, so they simply had everyone under surveillance for several months. They wanted to indict all of them simultaneously rather than approaching one member of the conspiracy with an offer of immunity in exchange for testimony against the rest of them. We are meeting with the Board of Trustees at 4:30. Can you come over to the University Club right now where we can talk privately?"

"Yes. I am on my way."

Matthews left immediately for the University Club, walking at his fastest pace. While he said nothing to Rose about the subject, his most prominent concern in this entire dreadful episode was Julia. Matthews really hadn't the time to sort out her role in this debacle, if any. Quite possibly, she had no part whatsoever, but he was concerned because of her career as an art historian and her connection to Barbara McGowan. Nevertheless, he had an awful, sinking feeling that she knew some of the artwork in the President's home was stolen.

When Matthews arrived at the University Club, Jean was waiting for him in the lobby. His face looked more tense than usual, and his hands were thrust deep into his trouser pockets creating an image of uncharacteristic stiffness. A movement of his head indicated, 'come with me.'

They immediately went to the third floor where George was waiting for them in a small, private conference room. Coffee, tea, and water were available at a small table, and Matthews picked up a bottled water and a glass, then took his seat at the small round mahogany conference table.

Georges began, "Garth we are terribly sorry to have kept you in the dark about this art theft investigation, but we were really given no choice by the F.B.I. I hate to tell you the reason, but I will. The F.B.I. at first believed that you might be implicated."

"In art theft?" protested Matthews. "I wouldn't know a Van Gogh from a Warhol. Actually, I would know the difference, but that would be the type of rudimentary knowledge I have about art."

"Yes, of course. More important, we told the F.B.I there would be no way that a person of your character would be involved in something so scandalous and immoral. But you will be flattered when I tell you the F.B.I.'s reasoning. They thought you might be involved because you have been a remarkably successful dean at the University. The agents assigned to the matter theorized you might be using dirty money to underwrite the meteoric rise of the law school.

For example, one of the agents thought you could be using the tainted dollars to provide extra scholarships for extremely talented applicants. Apparently, he was a college athlete. The same guy also thought you might be paying off-the-books rock star salaries to some of the faculty that you lured away from Harvard and Yale. Well, it didn't take them very long, however, to determine that you had nothing to do with this sordid scheme."

"When was this happening?" asked Matthews, thinking that the F.B.I. agents were damn good, because he had no idea he was under suspicion.

"That's not clear. Maybe a year and a half ago."

"Well, was this the end of it?"

"The F.B.I. ruled you out immediately. It was essentially a formality to even consider you." said Georges. Then, with a slight grin on his face, he continued, "But Karl and his conspirators thought that you had to have knowledge about their operation. You are the only dean at the University who can understand complex financial information, and you have frequently pointed out irregularities in financial documents. They also knew you could not be bought off if you discovered their plot," continued Georges. "Karl and his conspirators naturally were interested in finding out if you knew about their operation. It appears that a woman you were dating, Christine Knowel, approached Karl and offered to find out what she could about your knowledge of the operation of Karl's cabal. Of course, she wanted to be compensated. After making a deal with Karl, Christine did her best to insinuate herself into your life in order to keep track of your activities for Karl and the Finance Committee."

"So Christine Knowel was working for Karl?"

"Not from the outset. She approached them after you started dating."

"Am I still under investigation?"

"No, not at all, but Christine continues to be under constant surveillance by the F.B.I. When you were with her, you were definitely being watched. We are dreadfully sorry we couldn't tell you. Anyway, the agents assigned to this matter knew exactly what Christine was doing. They were even at the reception where you met. Of course, the fact she was being paid by Karl to report on you, made it clear to the F.B.I. that you were in no way connected to Karl's gang. Talk about an ironic twist."

"How long was I under surveillance?"

"Only days. They hardly opened a file. We think Interpol was involved too. We are not sure about the KGB, but we think they were watching you too. After all, Garth, we are talking about millions of dollars of artwork stolen from around the world. This matter involves a substantial number of paintings worth vast sums of money. This could be the largest amount of stolen artwork ever recovered.

"You also should be told that it is not clear whether this Christine woman has committed a crime. If her activities could be construed as part of the conspiracy, then she could be charged. If she was just providing investigative services, then no. One of the F.B.I. agents - I think it was Murphy - thought you demonstrated amazing restraint with Ms. Knowel. Believe me, you were lucky not to have become seriously involved with her. She has a history of doing some really bizarre stuff. She is not at all what she appears to be."

"Well, don't think I ever felt any real connection with her. She was oddly aggressive. Attractive, but clawing."

"It appears your instincts were spot on in her case," said Jean. "Also, we think you should leave Chicago tonight to avoid the fallout from this mess. As soon as it is announced that you are named the Interim President, the press will not leave you alone, and there is no way we want your appointment to be overshadowed by the news of the President's arrest. We have the permission from Agnes Schmidhausen to say that you are in New York to receive the Schmidhausen Leadership Award. We will have the press greet you at O'Hare when you get off the return flight from New York on Monday. Our P.R. people will prepare some speaking points, and we will run them by our lawyers. We have a delicate matter in dealing with tainted funds in our endowment, so this is one time when you will need to stay reasonably on script. We will handle the press here in Chicago while you are gone."

"Despite all of this distraction," said Georges, "You are still on board to be our Interim President, aren't you?"

"I gave you my word."

"Of course. So Monday you will step off the plane as the new Interim President and an award winner extraordinaire. Garth, I cannot tell you how grateful we are for you to step into this role during this crisis. Everyone in the community has total confidence in your integrity and ability, and if there is anyone who can navigate us through this mess, it's you."

"By the way," said Matthews, "do either of you know how much the cash award will be? I have been reluctant to ask, and no one from the Schmidhausen Foundation has told me."

"Actually, we do know," said Georges. "Agnes told us when we spoke with her, and she didn't tell us we couldn't tell you. I think she was a little tipsy when she spoke with us, but that is not unusual for Agnes. The cash award is just over twenty-four million dollars, tax free."

For a moment, Matthews felt slightly light-headed. He inhaled deeply. "Let me make sure I heard you correctly. You said twenty-four million dollars?"

"Yes. But you can check your Swiss bank account. The money should be there. Agnes said it was transferred earlier in the week."

"This is real money?" Matthews' head was so filled with information about corrupt activities, he could not help but ask. "I mean, it's not tainted in any way? The Schmidhausens are totally within the law? This is, ah, clean money?"

"Squeaky clean," replied Georges.

"Clean as clean can be," said Jean.

Matthews never had time to seriously weigh withdrawing from the process of consideration by the Schmidhausen Foundation. The award was his.

———

As Matthews walked back to his office, his cell phone rang.

"Garth, this is Christine."

"Christine! I thought I might be hearing from you."

"Garth, I owe you an explanation. I am sure you have heard by now that I was somewhat involved in this fiasco involving President Karl."

"Somewhat? It seems you were deeply involved, and you might be in trouble with the F.B.I."

"I am not in trouble with the F.B.I., I can assure you. Can I meet you to tell you about my involvement? It would make me feel better. Please."

"I am leaving the city, so this will have to wait." Matthews was not feeling inclined to be accommodating to Christine, having been told less than an hour before that she was being paid to interject herself into his life.

"I can meet you at O'Hare before your flight. You are flying out of town, aren't you?"

"Yes."

"Garth, it would mean a great deal to me."

"If it really means that much to you, I will. But I am sure we will be under surveillance when we meet. You know that, don't you?"

"Yes, of course. Can you meet me at four o'clock in the luggage pick-up area in the United terminal?"

"Christine, I will meet with you, but please understand that anything you tell me will not be confidential."

"I understand. I will see you at 4:00."

On his way to O'Hare, Matthews' cell phone rang.

"Dean Matthews," said the voice on the phone, "This is Jeanette Cartere. We understand that you will be coming to New York this evening. You will have a few days free to relax. That's good. It's no time for you to be in Chicago. I must say that the events at Lortigue University are quite extraordinary."

"Yes. Extraordinary."

"Just to let you know, the award will be announced on Saturday at 1:30 at a press conference at the Waldorf Astoria. All of the other details regarding the occasion will be in a binder which I will have delivered to your hotel. The reception at Mrs. Schmidhausen's apartment on Saturday will begin at 6:30. Dinner will be served no later than 8:00."

"Yes, I am looking forward to it, and I am glad to be out of Chicago for a few days."

"One more thing, Dean Matthews. I understand that Mrs. Schmidhausen has told Jean and Georges Lortigue the amount of the cash award. That should have never happened, but Mrs. Schmidhausen is getting a little forgetful as to protocols. And, as you might expect, she gave the Lortigues the wrong figure."

Matthews just sighed. He knew it could never be twenty-four million dollars.

"Dean Matthews, the correct number is forty-two million dollars."

"You said forty-two million, is that right?"

"Yes, forty-two million dollars and some small change. It is in your Swiss bank account now. I will send the confirmation of the deposit to your hotel and you can check your account on line. If you like, you can have the funds transferred to a domestic bank or an investment account at your convenience. But quite honestly, a Swiss bank account is about the safest place for your money until you make longer term plans."

"Thanks so much, Mrs. Cartere. I will see you on Saturday." Matthews once again felt light-headed at the thought of receiving an amount of money that had the potential of changing his life completely.

"Please remember the amount of the cash award cannot be disclosed to the public."

"Yes. Certainly." The amount of the award made him feel almost embarrassed. Of course, he would tell no one.

Matthews continued to ruminate about the award as the cab pulled up to the United Terminal. The thought became momentarily lost as he looked for the stairs to the baggage claim area on the lower level. He immediately spotted Christine who approached him as if she wanted to hug him. His body language clearly signaled that a hug was not welcome. Knowing that they were undoubtedly being watched, Matthews did not want anyone to infer that they were close. They shook hands.

Matthews purchased a coffee for each of them, and they sat next to one another on the connected vinyl-covered seats that are part of the motif of virtually every airport terminal in the United States. Forty-two million dollars kept re-emerging in his consciousness, and he did his best to suppress the thought in order to focus his attention on what Christine would tell him.

They each faced forward as Matthews waited for Christine to speak.

"Garth, I owe you an apology. I have deceived you several times, and I hope you can forgive me."

"Yes, you could have dragged me into something that would have been tremendously embarrassing – or worse."

"Garth, let me explain: To start with, while I am a lawyer, I have lied to you about my practice. I have never handled a major deal in my life, and the stories I told you about practicing law were fictitious. As you may know, I was being paid by Karl and the Finance Committee to become more deeply involved with you, and to find out what I could about your knowledge of their illegal activities. Actually, I approached Karl and told him that you knew of his misuse of University funds. I told him that I was unsure exactly how much you knew, and it would take time to get you to reveal the extent of your knowledge."

"It would seem to me that was reckless behavior on your part. You might be charged as a co-conspirator." Matthews tried not to sound judgmental, but given the facts, it was hard not to be disapproving in his tone.

"I guess that might be possible, but it is not going to happen."

"Why?"

"I supplied the F.B.I. with considerable information about Karl's operation, and I also provided information about their lunch meeting in order to ensure that they would all be arrested simultaneously."

"Who were you working for?"

"Myself and a European country I cannot disclose. Garth, the artwork involved in this matter is valued in the millions of dollars. I had to devise a way of infiltrating Karl's little group, and you were the means by which I was trying to accomplish this objective. I really did not want you to become collateral damage; I did my best to avoid that possibility."

"Thanks," said Matthews, with a touch of sarcasm in his voice. "Why didn't you just flirt with Karl and sleep with him?"

"Oh my God, Garth. Please," said Christine, shaking her head in disgust.

"I guess that question answers itself."

"I admit that would be the customary strategy, but in this case it was just not palatable. Sleeping with you, on the other hand, seemed like a very pleasant option. It didn't take me very long to decide which strategy I would choose."

"I'm flattered." This time the sarcasm in Matthews' voice was unmistakable. "Are you an agent for this European country?"

"I am what is sometimes called an 'independent' or 'free-lancer.' I work with different organizations such as the KGB, Interpol and the like. I have also worked for multinational corporations. I make a good living not because I am loyal to any particular country, but rather because I am good at what I do, and I can be depended upon to deliver the results that are requested."

Matthews continued to face forward, watching the luggage trundle along the conveyor belt.

"How can anyone trust you?" said Matthews, after a long pause, asking the obvious question.

"Actually, they can't. But I only get paid when I deliver results, and I have a very good reputation for being able to do that."

Christine sipped her coffee and continued with her explanation, "I was retained to find out as much as I could about the President and the Finance Committee. There were actually a number of ways to do that. I am sorry that I chose the strategy that involved you. Actually, when I was doing my research, my data on you was intriguing. I think I was trying to make my job more pleasant."

"You never thought I might be the person at Lortigue University who was engaging in unquestionable transactions?"

"Never."

"Never?"

"Please, Garth. You don't have a larcenous cell in your body. Anyone in my business could determine that immediately."

"So other than a few rather enormous lies about your career and the fact that you were trying to use me, what else do you need to apologize for?"

"I lied to you about the Schmidhausen family. And I actually provided false information to your lawyer, Ron Carey. I was working at his law firm only on a short term contract, a temporary position. President Karl arranged it."

"Why would you lie to me about the Schmidhausen family?"

"Mainly because I thought I needed to make you feel off balance by keeping your focus on the Schmidhausens. I didn't want you to start thinking about whether I was not what I claimed to be. It's a common tactic. And frankly, I was hoping to at least slow down the progress of your relationship with Julia. I actually feel very badly about that. You might be perfect for one another. I also feel badly about how things turned out between you and me."

"Our personal relationship? I am not sure we had one."

"No, I guess we didn't, but that was not my choice; it was yours."

"Yes…"

"Garth, in my kind of work it is rather commonplace for someone like me to sleep with men for whom I have no feelings. It's part of the job description. The female Russian spies are experts in these kinds of things, and I learned a lot working with two of them. Having sex with a man makes him vulnerable and needy. It is one of the most fundamental means of gaining control over a man. Its effect might not be long-lived, but it usually lasts long enough to get what I need, whether it is getting some information or getting him to do something like steal documents from his employer. In your case, I really didn't need anything from you. In actuality, it wasn't necessary for us to have a sexual relationship. It was only necessary that Karl believed we did. In truth, when I asked you to stay at my place, I just wanted to sleep with you."

"You weren't falling in love with me, were you?" For the first time during the conversation, Matthews glanced slightly at Christine.

"Oh, heavens no. We could never fall in love with one another. In fact, I know that if we had continued to date, you would have been able to see that I totally lack the feminine qualities you are looking for. My softer qualities are mostly a product of being a good actress."

"But I did like you…"

"That's a long way from falling in love. Actually, I liked you too. Very much. But with all the veneer stripped away, we would be a terrible match."

"I suppose so," said Matthews as he looked down into his coffee cup. He felt a slight sadness, not for himself, but for Christine. He momentarily wondered what events in Christine's life led her to her career. He quickly realized, however, he would never know.

"Thank you so much for letting me unburden myself. I just wanted you to know that I never meant in any way to hurt you."

Christine got up and walked away, leaving Matthews alone on the vinyl chairs with his coffee. While he wasn't sure, Matthews thought he saw tears well up in her eyes before she turned away. He watched the parade of luggage move along the conveyor belt for a few moments, and then he headed for his gate.

———

It was not until Matthews was seated in the first class cabin that he started to try to sort through his conversation with Christine. He wondered whether he would have allowed himself to be drawn closer to her had he not met Julia. He realized that this was another question that would be forever unanswered.

Matthews tried calling Julia once more before the plane pushed away from the gate. He had been trying to speak with her all day, but he had only reached her voice mail. It was hard to believe that he had seen her only last night. Since then he had been pummeled by body blows of one surprising fact after another. Matthews' thoughts were interrupted by Art Nelson, again in his navy blue suit and yellow paisley tie, who had just entered the first class cabin and sat down next to him.

"Dean Matthews, I guess you have had quite a day."

"Yes, I have. And how would you know that? Have you been watching the news about Lortigue University?"

"Yes, but I am also part of the team that was keeping Christine Knowel under surveillance."

"The team?"

"Oh, I am sorry. The F.B.I. team. I am Agent Nelson. I was assigned to maintain surveillance of Christine Knowel. Of course, we have known Ms. Knowel for some time. We have been watching her since you two met at the Lortigue reception. We had her under surveillance not because she was likely to do anything unlawful, but rather to further our own investigation of the president and the trustees at Lortigue."

"I am sure you know I just met with her. She is a fascinating person, but I can't help but feel that she is also somewhat tragic."

"She is very hard to figure out – rather a mystery. You want to know something? When you went to dinner at her house, I bet a senior agent that you would stay for the night. Thank God, I lost the bet. I am truly glad that you didn't. This senior agent told me that she wasn't your type. Frankly, I found that hard to believe because I thought she would be every guy's type."

"Art, that may be why I didn't stay." The insight of the remark eluded Nelson.

"I guess I have some maturing to do before I have the right instincts for these things. I thought she had done a remarkably cunning job in getting close to you. She's a real pro, I must admit."

"I really wouldn't know."

"Actually," replied Nelson, "I think she started to develop real feelings for you."

"I found her attractive, but Art, it wasn't happening for me, and I am lucky it wasn't."

"Damn lucky."

"I suppose you have been monitoring my behavior on these flights."

"No, not really. My assignment was to keep Christine Knowel under surveillance. We actually had a suspicion that she might be on this flight. I regularly volunteered for this duty. I have a girlfriend who lives in New York. I am on these flights all the time."

"It's none of my business, but are you pretty serious with this woman?" Matthews was not sure why he asked this question.

"Yes, we have been dating for three years. She's an agent in New York."

"Are you engaged?"

"No. I think I am just afraid to pull the trigger."

"Art, that's a really bad metaphor, although probably not an unusual one for an F.B.I. agent, I would guess," said Matthews with a cringe. "You really have to start thinking differently about marriage."

"Frankly, I just am not certain what type of feelings I should have to ask a woman to marry me."

"Art, the heavens are never going to open to release a flock of white doves carrying a banner with a message. You know, more realistically, it is kind of like when you were a kid and you finally dove off the high diving board. You've been thinking about it a long time. You may even go up the ladder and come down a few times. Then one day you just do it."

"That's a hell of a lot better metaphor than 'pulling the trigger,' I must admit."

A flight attendant's voice came over the speaker system, "Prepare for takeoff."

Matthews continued to speak over the elevated noise of the airplane engines, "You don't think I am an old guy living in the past, do you?"

"Oh, no sir. I think you are living very much in the present, not the past. We know you are very interested in Julia Nghiem. Now, my instincts are nothing like that of my senior colleague, but I bet you will spend a lot of time with her over the next few days."

"Your instincts are better on this one than on Christine Knowel."

"Dean Matthews, I really shouldn't give you this information, but I think I have complete deniability if the issue should ever come up. I believe Julia really cares about you. I think she started to fall in love with you before you two ever met. Honestly, she had a huge amount of documentation about you, and I think it helped her overcome her fundamental shyness about men. If she tells you she is shy about men, she is telling the truth. I am really overstepping my bounds here, but she may already be in love with you. And here is the part that is certainly none of my business, and that I surely should not be telling you. But Julia is the finest person you will ever meet. Her integrity is unlike that of any person I have met. You can trust her, I assure you."

"But how...?"

"We are the F.B.I. We know these things."

During the cab ride to the hotel, Matthews suddenly recollected that Jeanette Cartere had told him that his cash award would be forty-two million dollars. He was almost startled by the thought coming back into his consciousness and amazed that a thought like this could be displaced even temporarily by other matters. Now that he had some time to think about it, he did his best to begin to understand the magnitude of that amount of money. He had seen ads for houses in the Hamptons for twenty or thirty million dollars, but he would never want to buy such an extravagant residence. A large co-op or condo in New York could cost twenty-five million or more, but he would never want a place like Posse's, where Julia and he went as part of their first date. He wondered what disease could be cured for forty-two million. How much suffering could be eliminated by simply donating all of this money to one worthy charity? Interestingly, although there were no restrictions attached to the use of the cash award, the Schmidhausens expressed a desire that the award not be used for large charitable contributions. As explained in the materials Matthews received in the original binder from Jeanette Cartere, the Schmidhausen Foundation makes hundreds of millions of dollars in charitable donations every year, and the leadership award is meant to provide a reward to benefit the recipient for extraordinary achievements.

Matthews arrived at the Iroquois hotel around 8:30, somewhat fatigued by the extraordinary events of the day.

"Good evening Mr. Matthews, we are pleased to see you again," said the desk clerk. "You have had a number of things delivered here, and we placed them in the suite on the desk. I hope that's acceptable."

"Yes, of course."

"The chef has prepared a cold salmon plate that is in the refrigerator in your suite along with a salad and some desert. He thought you would want to eat in your room. But, of course, if you prefer, you can eat in the dining room."

"Actually, the salmon plate sounds fine. Have there been any messages?"

"Yes, a few. They are on the desk in your suite. John will take your bags to your room."

When Matthews entered his room, the binder from Jeanette Cartere was there as promised, and there were three envelopes with messages. One envelope contained a message from the Lortigue brothers thanking Matthews for his willingness to step in as Interim President. The Board of Trustees enthusiastically approved his appointment, with no dissenting votes at the 4:30 meeting.

The second envelope contained a note from Andy McAndrews, the first President of Lortigue University:

Garth,

I always wanted you to succeed me as President of Lortigue University. Perhaps that will now happen. Please know that I stand ready to provide any counsel, advice and support you might request. If anyone can lead us out of this sordid quagmire, you are the person.

Sincerely,

Andy.

The third was a handwritten note that had apparently been delivered to the hotel. It was from Julia.

Dear Garth,

I am so happy that you are safely in New York. I want to tell you that lying to you has been the hardest thing I have ever done, and I hope you can forgive me.

I will call.

Sincerely,

Julia,

'Lying to me?' said Matthews to himself. 'What the hell is this about?'

His cascading feelings of falling in love with Julia suddenly became choked off as he started thinking that his relationship with Julia might be as much of a charade as was his involvement with Christine Knowel. The last thing he wanted to learn was that he had developed very strong feelings for Julia as a product of some sleight of hand. Garth Matthews, for his entire career, was a man who was nobody's fool, and suddenly everyone around him was a fraud. He was actually starting to grow weary of new adventures and longed for a modicum of predictability in his life.

Three ice cubes; Macallan 18-year old; the crackling sound of the ice when covered by the Scotch, followed by the usual conditioned feeling of well-being. Nevertheless, the feeling was less intense then he had come to expect. He sipped the Scotch, telling himself not to jump to conclusions. Strangely, he thought back to his conversation with Art Nelson – Agent Nelson. The diving board emerged as an image in his mind, and he said to himself, "I am halfway up the freaking ladder with Julia, and this has all been some cunning trick."

After a few more sips of Scotch, he started to feel more calm. He told himself that he should not let his mind spiral uncontrollably. Another sip and he was starting to find some equilibrium.

He reached for his glass one more time, and then he saw the remote control for the television on the table. Pushing the buttons several times, he found the local news station. He turned up the volume.

"We are following a breaking story: We earlier showed the video of an arrest that occurred about an hour ago at Kennedy International Airport. We see here the security line at the Virgin Atlantic terminal. Two passengers bound for St. Petersburg, Russia were arrested and taken into custody. In this video they are being escorted by the NYPD and plain clothes officers believed to be F.B.I agents. No other arrests were made at this time, and we have been assured by airport security that these arrests are not terror related."

Well, those folks are having a bad day, thought Matthews, who took another sip of his Scotch and tried to relax.

The television news station broadcast some financial news, the usual report on random global warming, a story about an environmental disaster somewhere in the northern hemisphere, and then returned to the Kennedy Airport story.

"We have learned that the individual arrested is a prominent New York City resident known by the name of Henry Posse. He has also been known as Vladamere Potusky and Yakov Yodsky. He was flying on a one-way ticket with no checked luggage and was accompanied by a woman, possibly his wife. He had over six hundred thousand dollars in cash on his person at the time of his arrest. A warrant for his arrest was issued yesterday, but he had successfully eluded the authorities until this time. We understand there will be a press conference about the arrest in approximately seventeen minutes."

Posse! At this point Matthews became extremely frustrated trying to impose some order on the seemingly disparate facts that had recently occurred in rapid succession. Undoubtedly, he thought, they were all somehow connected. In his mind there was a blurred collage of images that seemingly could not have all occurred within the last twenty-four hours. But they had. He had been trapped in a cache of stolen artworks in the home of the President of his University with a woman he kissed and began to feel that he loved. He was fired from his position as Dean of the College of Law of Lortigue University, but in reality he was not, because the President who fired him, who was gorging himself at the time on a jelly donut, was later arrested. The President's arrest resulted in Matthews becoming appointed as Interim President. He learned that this same President of Lortigue University was corrupt, something that really did not surprise him, but he was astounded about how monstrously corrupt he actually was. He learned that he had been under surveillance by the likes of the F.B.I. and Interpol, and he learned that a woman whom he had dated was a secret operative for a European country. And it should not be forgotten that he thought he was to receive a cash award of twenty-four million dollars, but in reality it turned out to be forty-two million. All of this made some bizarre sense, but the part that he could not make fit was that Julia had lied to him. Julia had lied to him? About what?

Suddenly, it was déjà vu. On the television screen there was a blue curtain and the emblem of the F.B.I. A man appeared before the blue curtain.

"Good evening. I am Assistant U.S. Attorney Rodney Gorshin. Today we arrested Henry Posse who is also known as Vlademere Potusky and Yakov Yodsky. We have also arrested his wife on conspiracy charges. Her name is Lilly Tran. These individuals have allegedly bought and sold fifty-three pieces of stolen artwork over a period of twelve years. We have had Mr. Posse under surveillance for over seven years, but were only able to positively identify the stolen works of art recently. For those of you who have followed our announcement earlier today in Chicago, there is a connection between this case and the matter in Chicago involving the President of Lortigue University. We believe Mr. Posse was trying to flee the country after learning of the arrest of President Frank of Lortigue. The arrests will lead to charges under Title 18 of the United States Code, Sections 659, 2314, 2315 and 668.

"I would now like to introduce the team that worked on this case. They are all members of the F.B.I.'s Art Theft Program which was created in 2004.

Since its creation, the Art Theft Program has recovered millions of dollars of stolen artwork.

"To my left is F.B.I. Agent Robert Murphy."

Agent Murphy stepped into view alongside of Mr. Gorshin.

To his left is Special Consultant and Special Deputy F.B.I. Agent, Barbara McGowan from Chicago, and to her left is Special Consultant to the F.B.I. and Deputy F.B.I. Agent Julia Nghiem of New York."

Julia walked into view wearing her glasses and a dark grey suit.

"We cannot answer any questions at this time."

Matthews put three ice cubes in the glass and poured a second Scotch.

CHAPTER TEN

THURSDAY

MATTHEWS AWOKE AT ABOUT 7:00, went to the health club to work out, and returned to his suite to order breakfast.

He had slept restlessly the night before as the residue of Wednesday spilled over into his sleep. While he could only vaguely recall this imagery of his dreams, they were dominated by competing likenesses of Julia and Christine arguing with one another as to who had been the most clever in deceiving Matthews.

His breakfast arrived, and he drank about half the pot of coffee in order to clear his head. He realized that he should not feel legitimately cheated of anything after he learned that he had a windfall of millions of dollars. Nevertheless, he felt potentially deprived of something that meant much more to him than riches as he entertained the strong possibility that his relationship with Julia was over.

He picked up a magazine on the coffee table of his suite, New York Elegance, and flipped through the pages with pictures of beautiful people shopping for jewelry, clothes, cars and works of art. Matthews surmised he could now afford to purchase anything he saw in those pages, and while he understood that his life had changed for the better to an absolutely astonishing degree, the thought did not produce any real elevation of his spirits.

As he started to pick at the breakfast on his room service tray, Matthews had a dreadful feeling of inadequacy. He had failed to see what was obviously happening around him, and the very grip that he had on his life had been deceitfully pried away. The confidence that he usually felt in his ability to negotiate sophisticated situations, even risky situations, was being ripped away as he realized that he unknowingly had been under surveillance for over a year, that his best friends who knew about the surveillance could not tell him, and that he allowed one woman to enter his life through deceit, and another to enter his heart through subterfuge. Matthews could not help note the irony of his feelings at a time when he was about to receive a reward for outstanding leadership. His appetite for risk-taking had all but vanished. In its place, a sickening sense of witless ineptitude was rapidly developing.

Matthews looked at his newspapers. On the front page of The New York Times was a picture and story about the arrest of Henry Posse. He quickly read the story, but it made no mention of Julia. Rather the story focused on his nature of Posse's trafficking in stolen artwork and the potential recovery of paintings that had been hidden from the public for years.

His cell phone rang. Almost afraid to see who was calling, he answered the phone without looking at the screen.

"Garth, this is Julia."

"Hello Julia," he said, with a flatness in his voice

"I suppose you are angry with me."

"I honestly don't know what I feel."

"Well, I understand if you feel hurt and angry. It would be natural. I am extremely sorry that I have not been able to call you until now."

There was a long, awkward pause.

"Yes, I think I feel hurt, but I don't think I've gotten around to the angry part yet."

"Well, Garth, maybe I can prevent that from happening, if you give me a chance."

"How? You lied to me and let me develop feelings for you when it was all part of your very professional, and effective I might add, effort to keep me under surveillance."

"Garth, I never had you under surveillance. I am a consultant to the F.B.I., not some agent in a trench coat."

"You never had me under surveillance? You never tried to insinuate yourself into my life?"

"Definitely, 'no' to the first question. As to the second question, the most truthful answer is 'yes,' but not because I had any F.B.I. assignment to do that. Yes, I tried to insinuate myself into your life because I liked you, and I genuinely wanted to be part of your life."

"Our dates?"

"Our dates were real dates. I think the count is two dates, and they were wonderful."

"Our kiss?"

"Amazing. You don't think that the F.B.I. can teach a girl to kiss like that, do you? I didn't know that I could kiss like that."

A smile came across Matthews' face, but not because he was suddenly reassured. He wasn't. But Julia's ability to express herself in such a charming fashion was clearly one of her most alluring qualities.

"Well, what now?" said Garth trying to keep his defenses on the ready.

"Honestly, Garth, I would love to see you right away, but I have paperwork that must be completed at the F.B.I., and I have to teach two classes. Would you come to my place for dinner? Do you like Vietnamese food?"

"Actually, I do. Please e-mail the address and time. I must tell you, Julia, I feel very cautious about this. I think you should know that."

"I understand. I really do. I will send you an e-mail with my address."

Matthews sat quietly in his chair and tried once again to make sense of what was happening to him, both in his surrounding world and in his heart. While he could resolve very little, he knew he wanted to see Julia. And to pass the time until dinner, he decided to visit the Hayden Planetarium, a place where he was taken by his father when he was a boy whenever they visited New York City together. It was a wondrous place where clouds never obscured the night sky, and the stars could always be seen clearly.

—

Matthews took a cab to Julia's greystone on the Upper East Side. Not sure of the nature of the evening, he treated it as if it was a date, and accordingly, he was armed with a bouquet of mixed flowers and a fine bottle of 1993 Bordeaux.

Julia answered the door in bare feet, jeans and a white top that was like a T-shirt, only nicer. She seemed out of breath as if she had run to answer the door. An awkward moment passed, and she took the flowers and the wine from Matthews and laid them on the floor. She then slowly put her arms around his neck.

"Is this permissible?" she whispered in Matthews' ear.

"Yes."

Julia slowly pulled Matthews closer, and he responded by putting his arms around her back. In what seemed like minutes rather than seconds, their movements formed an ever tightening embrace.

"Garth," Julia whispered while still holding tight, "I am so sorry I had to lie to you. It wasn't my choice. I don't want to lose you; you must let me explain."

They released each other slightly and Julia pulled her head back in order to look at Matthews' face. She could see that tears were about to fall from his eyes, and seeing that, she started to weep openly.

"Oh my God, Garth, I have hurt you. I never would have wanted that. I would have told you right away, but I couldn't. I was not permitted to tell you that I was working with the F.B.I. I had to swear to it."

"I think I am just emotional because my feelings are so confused."

"Garth, I can explain everything. Please let me."

Pulling out his handkerchief and matting Julia's eyes, Matthews responded, "I am a better listener with something to drink."

"Of course. I usually don't have Scotch in the house, but I bought some on the way home from the Hunter. I actually bought two bottles in the hope that you will be coming here often."

Matthews really did not take in the beauty of Julia's home until she left to make drinks. While the furnishings were not distinctly of any specific type, there was a feeling that the room was both Asian and French Country. The balance of furniture and forms created a tranquil, serene space.

Julia reentered the room with a Scotch and a glass of white wine. She gave Matthews his Scotch and pulled a chair up to the couch where Matthews was seated. Their knees were practically touching.

"Garth, I almost don't know where to begin this explanation, but let's start with some of the fundamental truths and lies." She looked into his eyes directly, never averting her gaze. "I admit there were lies, but I had no choice. I'll tell you the truth about everything. First, my name is Julia Nghiem, and I am not a member of the Schmidhausen family."

"You are not a Schmidhausen? Is there a Mr. Nghiem?"

"Ah, yes."

"Yes?" said Garth, totally deflated.

"Yes, he is seventy-six years old, and he lives in Paris. He is my father. My mother lives there as well. Her name is Francine, and she is French."

Matthews realized that his questions were not helpful. He sipped his Scotch and decided not to interrupt Julia. But it became almost impossible.

"I am an Art History Professor at Hunter College, and what I have told you about my career there is absolutely true."

"Harvard and Yale?"

"Both true."

"Four years ago, I was approached by the F.B.I. to provide expert testimony involving the authenticity of two seventeenth century paintings. I actually enjoyed being an expert witness. The F.B.I. leaned that I had a photographic memory, and consequently, they realized that I could be of significant value to them. They retained me as a consultant, and they assigned me to work with Art Nelson who often posed as my boyfriend."

"Were you two romantic?"

"Garth, I have told you everything about the men I have dated," said Julia in a slightly dismissive tone suggesting that Matthews should be able to discern which facts were true and which were fabrications. "He posed as my boyfriend. Anyway, he is not my type, and he has a long-standing girlfriend."

"I know," said Matthews taking some minimal pride in having some inside intelligence.

"How do you know?"

"He told me on the plane yesterday."

Julia smiled, and then continued, "I actually found it very rewarding to work with the F.B.I. in recovering stolen art. It occupied much of my free time when I wasn't teaching or writing scholarship."

"And the Schmidhausens? How did you become involved with them?"

"About a year ago, when the process began to select the recipient of the Schmidhausen award, the Schmidhausen family had the need to consult the F.B.I. about a candidate from Virginia. Art Nelson was assigned to speak with Agnes Schmidhausen, but for some reason, Art and Agnes didn't have the best chemistry. Art thought that Agnes might be more comfortable talking to a woman, and he asked me to sit in on a few meetings. The matter was pretty perfunctory, but Agnes really liked going over the details in files. I think she considered it to be in the nature of gossip or eavesdropping. She and I had a good time laughing about the really idiotic things powerful people do. This investment banker in Charlottesville actually gave his social security number to someone over the phone when he tried to purchase male enhancement pills. He didn't do anything wrong. He just did something really stupid. Agnes thought that was one of the funniest things she ever heard. I can recall her saying, "What a dick!" and both of us couldn't stop laughing. Art just sat there trying to exhibit model governmental behavior."

"Well, wasn't that the end of your connection with the Schmidhausens?"

"You would think so, but it wasn't. Agnes and I became friends, and she asked me to serve as a trustee of the Schmidhausen Foundation. She said I had all the right credentials: I had advanced degrees from prominent universities, I had F.B.I. training, and I am from a prominent international family..."

"How prominent?"

"I guess I would say the equivalent of the Schmidhausens or the Lortigues."

Matthews suddenly made himself more conscious of his surroundings, and he realized that he was sitting in an Upper East Side greystone which had to have a price tag in the millions. But he didn't dwell on this fact. He was more eager to hear what else Julia had to say.

"Well, Agnes and I became quite close. She never had female heirs, and she would often introduce me as her granddaughter when we would go to social functions, you know, art show openings, charitable events. She has a son, of course, but they actually have a rather peculiar relationship. He lives in New York, but she rarely sees him. Can you guess where this is going?"

"I am not sure, especially as it relates to me."

"Well it became clear that in a true grandmotherly fashion, she was trying to introduce me to men. She wanted to be the matchmaker."

"Okay. I am almost there."

"I think you can connect the dots from here. I read your complete dossier for the Leadership Award as a member of the jury reviewing your dossier. I can remember gasping when I saw your picture, something which Agnes noticed immediately. And then about a month later, I spoke these fateful words at lunch with Agnes at the Waldorf: 'I wish I could find a man like Garth Matthews.' That was all Agnes had to hear. It seemed like from that moment, her life's work became putting us together, which in reality was not all that hard since at that point, you had already been selected for the Schmidhausen Award. Garth, the only thing I lied to you about was my status as an F.B.I. consultant and my connection to the Schmidhausens. Everything else has been the truth, especially what I have said about my feelings. Please believe me."

Matthews sat in stunned silence. It all made sense; it really did. But still his feelings had become numbed by repeated assaults of new information that made him question his ability to separate fact from illusion.

"Garth, here is the most important part, and if you give it any reflection, it will ring true. In fact, this is the lynchpin of the entire story that supports all of its disparate pieces: I am incredibly shy when it comes to men. I have told you this repeatedly, and it is absolutely true. There could be millions of men out there who might be suitable for me, but I could never know it. If I meet a man, he loses interest before I can let him close to me. While I want to be embraced, my immediate reaction is to cringe at the thought of being touched. And while I am often lonely and wish I had a partner, I am usually terrified by the thought of living with men that I have met. But I knew you before I met you, and that, if I had to submit design specifications for my soul mate, I could not have done a better job than who you are. Garth, please, I think I am in love with you, and it will rip my heart out if you don't give me a chance."

At this point, tears were streaming down Julia's face and her fists were clenched in fear that Matthews would not understand her or believe her. Her head was bowed in uncontrollable weeping. Recovering, she slowly looked up and wiped the tears from her eyes in a twisting motion of her curled hands, not unlike a child. She was afraid to look at Matthews, for fear that she would see rejection in his face. But as she blinked the final tears out of her eyes, she saw her made-to-measure man on his knees in front of her.

Matthews spoke quietly and deliberately, "Julia, I believe you, every word, and walking away from what we have would be heartbreaking for me too. Actually, my feelings for you are stronger than you can imagine. I have never felt so confused and perplexed as by what has happened to me over the last several days. The facts are so exquisitely intricate that I almost have no choice but to rely on my feelings. In fact, it's hard for me to understand the intensity of my feelings for you, because we haven't known each other for very long. But I know my feelings are very real. Julia, if this is going to work, however, you must understand that I am not the dossier or the F.B.I. file. I cannot be that perfect."

"Garth, I understand," she said sweetly. "I may be shy, but I am not immature."

They kissed intensely, and when they released each other from the embrace, Matthews acknowledged, "That was no F.B.I. kiss."

For the rest of the evening they spoke quietly to one another slightly above a whisper. They talked about how they each were lonely even though their individual lives were filled with interesting people and meaningful things to do. As Garth helped Julia with the cooking, they talked about the emptiness of taking vacations alone and the fear of some uncertain crisis that a simple person might have to face alone. They talked about their individual lives that were blessedly full, but nevertheless incomplete. And when Matthews left at eleven o'clock, neither would later remember precisely what they had said to one another, but each knew that the strength of their connection was undeniable.

CHAPTER ELEVEN

FRIDAY

A FTER RETURNING FROM THE health club and ordering breakfast, Matthews sat drinking his coffee and thought about his evening with Julia. In fact, it was impossible for him to think of anything else.

What puzzled him most was his urgent flood of feelings for Julia. He considered the possibility that it was a matter of timing in his own life triggered by his increased longing to find a partner. But he also considered even stronger the likelihood that Julia was simply different than other women he had met. She was undeniably beautiful, but not in a way that women are typically beautiful. A man could miss it at first glance, only later to be overwhelmed by its intensity. While her features were nearly perfect, more significantly, her face radiated a resplendent intricacy that was a perfect representation of her inner being. Consequently, as Matthews had come to understand her inner complexity, Julia became progressively more beautiful to him. He actually sensed this happening: Every time he saw Julia, she appeared more beautiful than the time before, making Matthews all the more eager to see her every time they planned to meet.

Julia was undeniably smart and accomplished. She expressed herself in a warmly captivating way that belied the underlying shyness to which she readily confessed. She was graceful, and Matthews took great pleasure in merely watching her move. Of course, she could be deadly serious, but she also had a remarkable playful side as well. After all, she was capable of performing confounding feats of magic.

After much reflection, Matthews decided that while he had been longing for a partner for years, that was not the dominant source of his attraction to Julia. What made this relationship so amazingly intense were Julia's extraordinary qualities. She deserved the credit that was due. She really was something unique. A wave of emotion washed over Matthews, and his eyes filled with tears as he realized how lucky he was. He also realized that his need for risk-taking may have been in large part a distraction from his loneliness or some odd sublimation of his need to connect deeply with a woman.

His breakfast had arrived and Matthews ate his oatmeal while flipping through the pages of the New York Elegance. His spirits had changed dramatically since the day before when he had done the same thing. As he looked through the pictures of beautiful clothes, antiques, automobiles, jewelry... Jewelry! He realized that he had not yet given Julia a gift. He immediately became energized by the prospect of selecting a piece of jewelry for her. He ripped a few pages out of the magazine, put them on the table, and then jumped into action to prepare himself for the mission.

Matthews decided to walk up Madison Avenue to find one of the jewelers from the pages of New York Elegance. A half block north of 61st and Madison, he found Angland Brothers, New York, Paris and London. An attractive blond sales associate greeted him, and a vague unsettling feeling immediately came over him. She reminded him of Christine.

The sales associate introduced herself as Charlotte, and with a smile and a few pleasant words, she erased Matthews' uneasiness. In fact, once they started talking about a possible purchase, Matthews found that she was quite pleasant.

"I am looking for a gift for my friend, my girlfriend," began Matthews. "This is the first gift I am giving her, and it is really not a special occasion."

"It becomes a special occasion if it's a first gift. I would say you are giving her a gift because you have become confident that you have real feelings for her."

"That's amazingly insightful."

"Not really. I've been in the jewelry business for seven years, and there is always a reason behind the purchase of a piece of jewelry. First gift – that's actually an easy one."

Matthews smiled. He thought about telling her that he was halfway up the ladder of the high diving board, but wisely decided against it.

"Let me suggest a bracelet. It's too early for a ring, and actually, you never want to give your girlfriend a ring box before you are ready to have a diamond in it. A necklace is nice, but it's a bit tricky. Women have definite ideas about what they wear around their necks, and you could miss the mark by a wide margin. A pin or broach is out ever since Madeline Albright made a big deal about wearing them. If your girlfriend happens to be Madeline Albright, then it would be fine. But I think I can safely assume that is not the case. A bracelet, however, is really an intimate piece of jewelry, more personal and private than other forms. A woman can keep it hidden if she wants to, and she will also wear it almost every day if she loves you – that is until you give her another one."

"I am convinced. What do you suggest?"

"Well let's stay away from birthstones and go more for what you think would be nice on her. To be honest, it might help if you tell me about how much you would like to spend. We try to avoid that question, but honestly the range here is enormous."

"That really doesn't matter," said Matthews who suddenly realized that he was acclimating to his status as a millionaire.

"Let's do this: We will pick out something nice, but something that does not appear that you are trying to impress her."

"You're clairvoyant."

"Seven years in the business…"

Ultimately, Matthews selected a diamond and sapphire bracelet. It probably was more expensive than the sales associate had anticipated, and it may have shaken her confidence in her ability to read customers. But in fairness, she had probably never encountered a customer who had recently fallen in love and became a millionaire almost simultaneously.

—

Julia had classes and a faculty meeting on Friday, and consequently, she and Matthews could not see each other until the evening. After shopping for Julia's gift, Matthews spent most of the afternoon in his suite conferring by telephone with the Lortigues, reading and answering e-mails, and catching up on paperwork he had brought with him. While Matthews had spent a good deal of time away from the management of the law school, he knew that Rose would not let anything spin out of control in his absence.

Matthews learned from Rose that the records she and Bea White had accumulated on suspicious transactions by the Lortigue Foundation had proven to be very helpful to the F.B.I. The Chicago newspapers were full of stories about the scandal at Lortigue University, and according to Rose, there had been a great deal of speculation as to who would be asked to assume the Presidency of the University. Rose told Matthews that his name was mentioned frequently, but much of the speculation centered on the possibility that the Lortigue brothers would run the University until the situation stabilized.

Matthews and Julia planned to meet for dinner at a restaurant at 73rd and Second Avenue called Bistro Carvande. Matthews arrived before Julia and rather than being seated, he strategically positioned himself for a full standing embrace. When Julia arrived she jumped to hug him, and Matthews was ready to catch her. They hugged tightly, and Matthews playfully lifted her feet off the ground as he arched his back slightly. It was a special moment: This was the first time they had greeted one another when they mutually understood the real nature of their feelings for one another. Casual observers might have guessed that they were lovers who had been apart for too long, and time being relative, they would not have been wrong.

"Garth, I have had the most wonderful thoughts about you all day," Julia whispered while still being suspended.

Matthews gently lowered Julia to her feet, "That's funny; I've had the same experience thinking about you."

The hostess patiently stood with menus in hand as Julia and Matthews whispered to each other. She waited to seat them until they both turned toward her and Matthews said, "We're done."

Once seated, Julia began the conversation. "Garth, people at the college actually noticed a difference in me today. I can't believe it. They told me I looked especially happy, and most of them attributed it to the arrest of Posse. It's been all over the local news. Most of my colleagues did not know that I was consulting with the F.B.I. I am so glad that is over. I'm not sure I am going to continue to work with them. I don't mind providing expert testimony, but I really don't like the field work looking at collections for stolen pieces."

"I can understand that. When we visited Posse's residence, was that the only time you actually saw his collection?"

"Yes, but of course I had some intelligence as to what to look for. The same was true for the President's collection - I should say the former President Karl's collection. By the way, Barbara McGowan told me today that he hasn't been able to post bail as yet. I think the judge set a phenomenally high amount because of the flight risk."

"I suppose he is going to do some serious time."

"Yes. I am sure. They all will."

"You know that I had dated a woman who was instrumental in their arrest"

Julia looked down, "Christine? Yes, I know that you were dating her when we met."

"Julia, I never…"

"I know. I actually know more than I should, but people in the F.B.I. are just human."

"Art Nelson?"

"Yes, of course. Long ago, he became like a big brother to me, even though he actually is younger. He would call me and tease me with phony code phrases."

"Like what?"

"Well, when you left Christine's apartment after dinner he said something like: 'No spark with art shark.' I can't really remember - I was so relieved. Art kept trying to assure me that, even if you slept with her, it didn't mean anything. Did you like her? Christine?"

"I don't think that is really the issue. At first, she seemed pleasant enough, but when it came to romantic feelings, it just wasn't happening for me. There was something about her that just did not seem genuine."

Suddenly, Julia seemed distracted, and then she smiled, "Garth, you'll never guess…"

Art Nelson--Agent Nelson--was approaching their table, and he sat down next to Julia whose back was to the wall.

"Act like we are old friends and smile. Garth, shake my hand," said Art in a hushed tone. Matthews complied. "Julia, don't appear to be upset or alarmed. Act natural."

Julia did her best, trusting Art completely.

"Now we will just chat to catch up on old times," said Nelson. "Garth, don't turn around, but Julia, if you look to the line of tables on the left wall of the restaurant, you will see a woman sitting by herself at the third table from the front."

"Yes, the blonde, in the low cut dress, with rather large breasts."

"You've spotted her. Garth, resist the temptation to turn around and look." Nelson was doing a splendid job acting as if he was just having a pleasant conversation.

"Well, my friends," continued Nelson, "that is none other than Christine Knowel."

Matthews' face blanched.

"She arrived in New York this morning. Not surprisingly, Garth, she has been following you, ever since you left the hotel to walk up Madison to the jewelry store. Oh crap…"

"What?" said Julia.

"I think I just spoiled a surprise. Julia, disregard where Garth went. Anyway, where was I? Oh yes. I've been watching her since you met her, Garth, at that cocktail reception at the University. I am really not sure why she is tailing you."

"What should we do, Art?" asked Julia.

"At the moment, nothing. I have been watching her for months, but am certain she does not know who I am or that I have been following her. I came over to your table because she began fumbling around in her purse. It's my guess that she picked up a weapon here in New York. She checked into the Regency, and I suspect she had it delivered to her room. I think that she is telling herself to wait until I leave the table but her patience will run out."

Matthews felt that Nelson's concern was unwarranted, but he resisted the impulse to turn his head to see if it really was Christine.

The waiter approached their table, and they each ordered a drink, acting as casually as possible.

"When the drinks come," said Nelson, "Christine will realize that I am going to sit for a while with you. At that point, she will either leave or approach us. If she approaches us, just don't do anything."

"Art, I think you are over-reacting. Christine may be somewhat outside the lines, but she would have no reason to harm us," said Matthews fearful that he might have sounded like he was defending Christine in front of Julia.

The drinks arrived, and Matthews asked Nelson, "Why don't you go over and introduce yourself?"

"I am afraid that if I do, she will pull out a gun and start shooting. Any number of people here could get hurt. If I wait, and if I am correct that she doesn't know who I am, I can easily catch her off guard and take her down from a standing position."

Julia started to appear to be frightened, and Matthews said to her, "Julia, first get yourself out of the line of sight by moving slightly to your right. Your face will be blocked by the back of my head."

"Okay, she is getting up," said Nelson, "And she is heading toward our table."

Julia appeared to be terrified but she sat frozen as Nelson had instructed.

Nelson stood up as the woman approached the table with her hand in her purse.

"Art, I just wanted to meet you since we have spent so much time together. It's been fun watching you follow me. Now that this caper is essentially over, I thought I would introduce myself. Here is my card if you want to contact me," said Christine removing a business card case from her purse. "Perhaps we could work together sometime."

"I suppose we could," said Nelson with a weak smile.

"Well, I certainly don't want to intrude," said Christine, "I just thought that since our business brought us all to the same place, I should say 'hello.' It is good to see you, Garth. And this must be Julia."

Julia stood up and extended her hand which Christine politely shook. Julia demurely smiled and gave Christine a 'He's mine, bitch' look. While, actually, Julia would never use those words, Christine had no trouble interpreting Julia's expression. Matthews was completely oblivious to the subtle dynamics between the two women, and Art Nelson just stared at Christine's ample breasts, this being the first time he had such an opportunity at close range.

"I actually know a great deal about both of you," said Christine, referring to Matthews and Julia, "I sincerely hope it works out for both of you."

"Christine," said Matthews, "Were you following me today?"

"Yes, I was."

"Why?"

"Just to stay in practice."

"Really?"

"Well, no. I frankly wanted to know what Julia looked like. It's a female thing."

Christine returned to her table and resumed eating her dinner.

"Well that was certainly unnerving," said Julia. "Art, why did you think she was going to harm us. I mean really; you scared me terribly."

"I'm sorry," replied Art who stood up to leave, "I guess I just don't understand women."

Matthews looked at Art and nodded, "It takes some seasoning. There is no F.B.I. training for that."

After profuse apologies, Art left Matthews and Julia to have their dinner.

"Well," said Matthews after Art left, "It's obvious that having dinner here is simply not a good idea. I think the ambience has changed completely."

"Completely," agreed Julia. "Let's leave as quickly as possible."

Matthews left cash on the table, more than enough to cover the drinks and a gratuity. He and Julia discretely exited the restaurant, with Matthews giving a polite wave to Christine.

Once outside, Matthews said rather playfully, "Would you like to have a virtual sleepover?"

"Well actually, I would like to have a real sleepover. Let's go back to your suite at the hotel. I have no food at my place, and I hate to admit this, but I am hungry. We can order room service and watch a movie. I can fall asleep on your shoulder. And, while I don't think this is the night we will make love, I will let you touch my breasts."

Matthews started to laugh. "What in the hell brought that up, not that I wouldn't love to touch your breasts."

"Well, that Christine woman has gigantic breasts. I just don't want you to feel that you missed out on anything."

"I never touched them, I swear."

"Never?"

"Never. Well, I may have brushed up against them one time, but touched them, never."

"No?"

"No, never."

Julia and Matthews took a cab back to the Iroquois Hotel, and after they dead-bolted the door of the suite, Julia seemed to relax.

"That settles it. No more F.B.I. work for me," said Julia.

"Probably a very smart decision."

"Can I borrow something to wear?" asked Julia removing her dress.

Matthews looked in his luggage and found a folded blue oxford cloth shirt and a pair of boxer shorts which he offered Julia.

"Perfect," said Julia taking them with her into the bathroom. She emerged looking incredibly cute in the shirt, the tails of which reached to her knees.

Garth was wearing a tee shirt and boxers, and Julia noticed that their shorts matched.

"You get them three in a pack. Frankly, they are not something guys take much time to pick out."

"Well from now on, let me pick them out for you, not that there is anything wrong with these."

"Oh, speaking of picking something out, I bought you a gift today."

"But why?"

"No reason… Actually, that's not true. There is a very important reason." Matthews slowed the pace of his voice and spoke in a whisper. "I bought you this gift because despite all the bizarre events in my life since I met you, there is one thing I am absolutely clear about: My feelings for you are profound and real…"

Julia started to cry. Matthews thought that he must have reached a new plateau of maturity because he understood why she was crying. A woman crying was once something that mystified him, something that was impossible to interpret. When it happened, he was never quite sure if he did something wrong or he did something right. In this case, it was clear to him that he had done something right, and he sat next to Julia on the couch and let her cry on his shoulder.

Wiping her eyes with the sleeve of Matthews' tee shirt, she stopped crying. "Can I open the gift?"

"Of course."

Julia slipped off the ribbon and removed the silver paper wrapping. Inside the cardboard outer container was a velvet-covered box with the usual spring hinge. Julia gently and slowly opened the lid of the velvet box and stared at the bracelet.

"Oh Garth, it's the most beautiful bracelet I have ever seen." She spoke in a whisper as if it were a secret. "I will wear it every day."

Matthews was delighted that Julia liked the bracelet, and he was particularly happy that the largest purchase that he made since becoming a millionaire was a gift for Julia.

After eating dinner from room service and sharing a bottle of wine, Julia and Garth did not watch a movie. Instead they continued their conversation in bed, facing one another with their heads on their respective pillows.

As Garth's eyes acclimated to the darkness, he was able to see Julia's face, and he touched her cheeks gently with his fingertips as they talked. They shared their memories of when they each were children. Garth told Julia about visiting the Hayden Planetarium with his father. He told her how his mother taught him to cook after he asked her for lessons. Julia told Garth about visiting the Louvre with her father when she was only five years old, and how she became intrigued by the lives of painters. She also told Garth about the Robert-Houdin Museum of Magic in Blais, France and the Musie de la Magi near the Isle Saint-Louie in Paris. Both of her parents helped her with her interest in performing magic because they thought it would help her overcome her shyness. Julia and Garth talked about plans to visit Paris, and then almost simultaneously, they both fell asleep.

When Garth awoke briefly in the night, Julia's head was on his shoulder, her arm was across his chest, and he realized that no one had slept beside him for years. He fell back to sleep feeling that their intimacy had grown more deeply even though they never kissed. Of course, he would have gladly responded to any overture from Julia, but he could tell the time had not yet come.

CHAPTER TWELVE

SATURDAY

G ARTH AWOKE BEFORE JULIA and quietly left her a note that he was at the health club working out. When he returned to the suite, Julia was in the shower.

When she opened the door of the bathroom, she was clad in at least three, if not four, towels.

"Don't worry, I left one towel for you," she said to Garth who was sitting in a chair wearing a cloth hotel robe and reading the newspaper. Garth calculated that their life together would be defined by this ratio: Four for Julia, and one for him. It was a ratio with which he would be glad to live.

"Did you find my note?"

"Yes. And I was very disappointed. I had planned to make love with you this morning, but now the moment has passed."

"No, you didn't. Besides, I wasn't in the mood," Garth said. He paused for a moment, and then smiled at Julia, "We are both lying."

"Teasing is not lying," said Julia kissing Garth's lips with her mouth slightly open. "I will never, ever lie to you again. But I will tease you mercilessly at least once a day. You know, it is possible that I could have been seduced."

"Okay, enough teasing." Of course, Garth was totally enjoying it. "I am afraid we have some serious business today."

Garth started thinking about what he would say at the press conference and the dinner. It was actually a difficult assignment: He was receiving an extraordinary award for leadership, but he didn't want to dwell on his own attributes and achievements. On some reflection, he decided that he might be over-thinking the entire matter.

Julia walked over to his chair and kissed him again a bit more passionately than moments before, and Garth was positively aroused by the fragrance of her shampoo and body wash. He had almost forgotten the aroma of a woman after she has taken a shower.

"Garth, I need to go to my place to change for the press conference. I will meet you at the conference."

⁓

Garth arrived for the press conference early, but not early enough to precede Agnes Schmidhausen and Jeanette Cartere, both of whom were drinking gin and tonics. He embraced each of them.

He took Agnes aside and told her, "I am indebted to you for introducing me to Julia. Of course, I am grateful for the Award, but I hope you understand that Julia really is the best part of this experience."

Agnes replied, sharp as ever, "And here I thought you were saving it all for me, big fellow."

They both burst out laughing, and Garth hugged her again. "You are more than I can handle, Agnes; I'll have to settle for Julia."

At that moment, Agnes and Garth formed a bond that they both cherished for years. Never a week would go by without Garth calling her two or three times just for the fun of exchanging smart comments. Agnes would often ask "Have you dumped that Julia yet? You know I can't live forever waiting for you." Actually, Garth was really checking on Agnes because he truly cared about her and was forever grateful for the role she played in his life.

The press conference was very routine. Fortunately, the major networks were represented, and video would be shared with Chicago affiliates. Garth displayed the perfect combination of modesty and dignity.

—

Garth arrived for his dinner at Agnes' apartment with Julia on his arm. He thought they were arriving promptly on time, but all of the other guests arrived previously as if it were a surprise party.

Jean and Georges Lortigue were there. To Matthews' complete surprise, they both had escorted Rose to the party. Jean had told Agnes that it would not be a real celebration for Garth without Rose in attendance, and he had indeed gauged Garth's feelings precisely.

Andy McAndrews, the first President of Lortigue University had come from Arizona with his wife, Gladys. His three closest friends from the faculty were there. He had felt that with all the recent distractions, he had been neglecting their respective friendships, and he was incredibly delighted to see each of them. He also realized that his romantic relationship with Julia would be no secret at the law school, and Garth introduced Julia to each of them.

Agnes' son, Hans Schmidhausen, introduced himself to Garth and Julia, and Garth expressed his sincere gratitude for the award.

Finally, Jeanette Cartere, accompanied by a distinguished-looking gentleman, appeared from another room and ran to hug Garth and Julia. Yes, of course, she was quite soused, but Garth really would have been disappointed if she were any other way.

"Let me introduce my husband," Cartere said, tugging on the gentlemen's arm, "Garth Matthews and Julia Nghiem, this is Sir Graham Wooleyfin."

"The renowned economist!" said Garth, to the surprise of everyone listening.

"Yes, I am. Well, I don't know how renowned I am, but I am an economist."

"You are the last recipient of the Schmidhausen Award," continued Garth, again to the astonishment of those in earshot. "I am delighted to meet you." He almost said that he was glad to see him alive, but he caught himself.

"Yes. Yes. That I am."

Cartere spoke up, "Well, you see, after Sir Wooleyfin received the Award, we, ah, well, we fell in love. Wooley and I have been together ever since." She gave Wooley a sloppy, very tonguey, kiss. Wooleyfin seemed embarrassed and wiped his mouth with his hand.

"Thankfully, Agnes gave us her blessings," said Wooleyfin. "You see, Agnes places a higher value on love than on leadership."

"That's good to know," said Garth, and he squeezed Julia's hand, who clutched his firmly in return.

"I still publish articles under a pseudonym," offered Wooley, almost apologetically. But Jeanette keeps me quite busy."

"I bet she does," said Garth with a smile, which Wooley returned with a wink.

The reception was in every way a spectacular event. A string quartet played the evening through. Guests spontaneously proposed toasts, and by dinner only Garth, Julia and the string quartet were sober. Actually, the viola player had more than his share, but it hardly affected him.

The dinner was a feast of seven courses, accompanied by a perfect wine for each course. And when it came time for Garth to give his speech, everyone at the table took turns interrupting him with words of praise. Garth was able to weave in the rope trick he had purchased at Tannen's, to the delight of everyone, especially Julia who did not know that he had been secretly practicing. When the speech was over, no one was quite sure what Garth had said. Even Garth was not sure what he had said. The words were hardly as important as the gathering of Garth's closest friends. Garth felt he loved everyone at the table, even Wooley, because Garth was just glad that he was alive. Julia, of course, did not interrupt Garth's speech as others had, but silently sat and realized that her admiration for Garth was equaled by others who had no hope of experiencing the intimacy that she would have with him. She actually understood and admired every word he said.

After dinner, Agnes played the piano and everyone raised their uninhibited voices in song. There were no song sheets, so occasionally the lyrics became muddled. But nobody really cared because Agnes sang more loudly than anyone else, and people just hummed as Agnes carried them through the song.

At one o'clock the party started to disassemble. Wooley and Cartere left first, with Wooley winking at Garth, and Garth nodding back in knowing understanding. He wasn't sure that he was comfortable with this arguably sexist male bonding, but he felt congenial to Wooley. Within minutes, everyone had left, leaving Agnes, Julia and Garth alone.

"Well," said Agnes, "I made it through the evening without fainting. And there has been more going on at this party than anyone realized."

"And why is that?" asked Garth.

"I don't suppose anyone noticed, but my son, Hans, disappeared about halfway through the party."

"Yes, come to think of it, I didn't see him leave," said Garth.

"Oh, he didn't leave. He's still here. Before this party, I hadn't seen him at all for months. Quite honestly, he is a terrible son."

"I'm sorry," said Julia, realizing at least partially why Agnes quickly adopted her as a granddaughter figure.

"He is such a disappointment. His father would be ashamed of him," said Agnes shaking her head in disgust.

"I am very sorry to hear that," said Garth. "Is it just his distance that disappoints you?"

"Oh my God. I could deal with that, but it is worse than just his refusal to see me. Would you like to say goodbye to him. You won't be seeing him for a long time."

"Yes, I really should thank him again for the award."

"Very well," replied Agnes as she led Garth and Julia down the hall to a bedroom. She opened the door to a bizarre but somewhat comical sight.

Hans Schmidhausen was seated in a chair in his underwear and black calf length dress socks. His arms were restrained by duct tape which kept his wrists anchored to the arms of the chair. His ankles were restrained in the same fashion, and a strip of duct tape covered his mouth. He struggled futilely to release himself.

"He has been a very bad boy," said Agnes. "I simply lost patience with his bad behavior. You see, at some point after his third divorce, he became bitter and hardened. Worse yet, he thought he was actually running the

Schmidhausen operation, something we leave to the experts here in New York and Zurich. He actually tried to invest our resources in illegal enterprises, like counterfeit pharmaceuticals. I had three of our top people undoing every transaction he made, in the hope we could rehabilitate him. When he tried to involve our orphanage in Viet Nam in sex trafficking, that was when I needed to put a stop to his actions. I realized that he could do serious damage and that we couldn't continue to handle this matter in-house. I think he just lost his mind, but he is a real danger to society. What a disappointment."

"But Agnes, why didn't you just have him arrested?" asked Garth.

"Our consultant advised otherwise."

"How did you get him restrained?" asked Julia.

"It was done between the third and fourth course of dinner."

"You did this by yourself?" asked Garth.

"No, I had some help. Ms. Knowel, you can come out now."

Christine Knowel emerged from the bathroom wearing incredibly tight black jeans and a revealing black halter top. In her hands she had a role of duct tape which she tossed from hand to hand as if it were a basketball.

"As I told you, Garth," said Christine, "In my line of work sometimes you have to be nice to men who are actually disgusting to you. Repulsive as it was, this was not a difficult case. Hans liked to be restrained. It just didn't end this time the way he likes it."

Hans Schmidhausen twitched and struggled to no avail.

Garth asked Christine, "How long have you been working for the Schmidhausens?"

"Less than a week. You see, after I received reports from my contacts in Europe, I realized that the Schmidhausens had a real problem that needed attention. Hans' activities were really starting to tarnish their reputation. I volunteered my services to Agnes in order to clean up this mess."

"Ms. Knowel has been extraordinarily helpful, and she has refused to accept a fee which we would have gladly paid to have this problem totally fixed," said Agnes.

Agnes ripped the tape off Hans' mouth and asked him to say goodbye to his guests.

He feebly muttered, "It's been a pleasure."

Agnes quickly replaced the tape over Hans' mouth, and said, "Hans, you have given me no choice. The authorities will be here shortly. Christine has already contacted them."

Christine said specifically to Garth and Julia, "Would it just be the most delicious irony if they sent Art Nelson?"

"Yes, it would," said Garth, "But I am afraid we are not going to stay to find out."

Garth had seen enough of a man in his underwear struggling and twitching like a trapped rodent.

As they left the bedroom, Garth could only imagine what torture Hans would have in store before the authorities arrived. While he was not sure about such things, he imagined that after a woman had sex with a man she found repulsive, there had to be some nasty acting out. Clearly, Christine was up to the task. But, thought Garth, Hans might actually enjoy it.

As Julia and Garth approached the exit to leave Agnes' apartment, Garth said "This will be an evening I will never forget."

"Nor I," added Julia.

Agnes said to Julia and Garth, "Of all the things I have done in my life, you two are my finest accomplishment."

Garth replied, "What about Jeanette and Wooley?"

"I had nothing to do with that. Wooley accomplished that on his own, the horny toad."

As Julia and Garth rode down the elevator to the lobby, Julia asked, "Why do you suppose that Christine woman volunteered to help Agnes?"

"I'm not sure," replied Garth, "but I think it had more to do with you than you might realize."

"Me?"

"Yes. I think she really believed that you were Agnes' granddaughter, and she wanted to do something nice for you, and indirectly for me."

"Really?"

"Yes, that would be my guess. She has a rather tough exterior, but I think she felt badly that her intrusion into my life may have had the potential of destroying something very real between you and me. But then, maybe she was bored and wanted something to do."

"And you are sure you never touched her breasts. I mean, they are rather remarkable."

"No. Never."

"Never?"

"Never."

Julia and Garth took a cab to the Iroquois where Julia had sent a suitcase earlier in the day. They sat quietly in the cab holding hands. Garth felt he was the luckiest man on the planet, and objectively speaking, no one could prove him wrong.

"Garth," said Julia during the cab ride, "It was a wonderful evening. I just didn't expect it to end the way it did."

"I don't think Hans thought it was going to end that way either. I am sure he expected it to end more happily."

When they arrived at the suite, Julia's luggage, which had been delivered to the room, was sitting on a stand in the bedroom. Ignoring it, she went into the bathroom and found Garth's oxford blue shirt and boxers hanging on the hook on the door.

When she came out of the bathroom, she found Garth dozing off in the chair.

"Garth, wake up. I need my Schmidhausen man to hold me while I sleep on his shoulder."

And they fell asleep in the bed with Julia's head on Garth's shoulder, her arm across his chest, and her left leg over his.

CHAPTER THIRTEEN

SUNDAY

G ARTH AWOKE FIRST AND gently rolled away from Julia's embrace. Julia showed no signs of stirring. They had fallen asleep late, but Garth was still surprised when he looked at the clock: It was nearly ten in the morning. He considered the possibility that he had finally relaxed after several days of extraordinary intensity.

Garth had a feeling that this day was an emotional oasis. He and Julia had the day totally to themselves. He did not have to fly back to Chicago until tomorrow, and time on this day was an irrelevant factor. Garth stealthily went into the bathroom, took a shower and shampooed his hair. He brushed his teeth and scrubbed his tongue with his toothbrush. He would have shaved, but he was afraid that the electric razor would awaken Julia. He put on a clean tee shirt and boxers, and crawled back into bed. He looked at Julia sleeping, and faithful to the pattern that was now well established, Julia looked more beautiful than ever before. He wanted to touch her face, but he restrained himself. As he watched her awake, he understood that he was witnessing something that happened every day that was in fact quite commonplace. But to Garth, it seemed magical.

Garth noticed that Julia was about to open her eyes, and respectfully, he closed his eyes so as not to make her feel uncomfortable. But he moved slightly to let her know that he was awake.

"Garth," she whispered, "It's almost ten-thirty. Do we have anything we have to do today?"

"Well, yes and no." He opened his eyes and looked directly into hers. "The 'yes' relates only to you and me. The 'no' refers to everyone else in the cosmos."

"Garth, your hair is damp. Did you take a shower?"

"Yes."

Julia immediately jumped out of bed and went into the bathroom. The shower ran. She returned in minutes. As she walked in front of the bed with not even one towel cloaking her body, Garth appreciated for the first time how perfect her body was.

"Okay, now we both have damp hair," she said, playfully massaging his scalp.

Garth became almost overwhelmed by the fragrance that emanated from Julia.

"Julia," Garth said looking into Julia's eyes, "Tell me what's going to happen now."

"Garth, you are going to look into my eyes, and we will not speak for minutes. We will just study each other's faces. Then I will kiss you gently on your mouth when I am ready. Our tongues will touch. And then I will put my hand behind your neck and I will pull you into my breasts. We will kiss some more, and you will hold me around the small of my back. And then when I feel I am ready, I will put my leg between yours, and I will feel on my leg that you are ready. And then it will happen. Exactly how, I don't know, but I will guide you so that you don't hurt me. And our mouths will always stay close."

Julia, for all of her lack of worldly experience, was exactly right. It happened precisely as she described.

———

Over time, Julia found that Garth had many extraordinarily endearing qualities beyond those identified in his dossier. The deepening of her love for Garth involved surprise and discovery, and their intimacy grew beyond anything Julia could have imagined from the first time she saw his picture.

Garth found Julia to be more beautiful not only each time he looked at her face, but also each time she revealed her soul to him.

Garth's penchant for taking risks no longer dominated his life. He did, however, continue to have an appetite for adventures, but only if they involved Julia. As to Texas Hold'em, Garth taught Julia to play the game, and given her extraordinary memory and intelligence, she became a more highly ranked player than Garth.

Julia and Garth were simply perfect for one another, blessed with a love that was ordained by the most transcendent of cosmic forces and a most marvelous grande dame named Agnes Schmidhausen.

EPILOGUE

CHRISTINE KNOWEL FINISHED HER assignment with the Schmidhausen operation. She never sent Agnes Schmidhausen a bill, even for her out-of-pocket expenses.

Hans Schmidhausen, represented by counsel, arranged a deal with a New York judge to be institutionalized in a psychiatric facility. He writes letters to Christine Knowel daily, which are never sent. Hundreds of such letters have accumulated in his file.

Art Nelson married his long-time girlfriend from New York and never regretted the decision. They have two children and a German Shepherd. Whenever the family goes to the swim club, Art demands that his wife watch him as he dives off the high board. She never fully understood why, but is glad to comply.

Georges Lortigue married Gerta, the Swiss woman, and Garth and Julia attended the wedding in Geneva. It was, not surprisingly, a lavish event.

Jean Lortigue began a beautiful friendship with Rose at Garth's celebration dinner. They were married a year later. Garth greatly missed working with Rose, but like Agnes, he felt that love was paramount. He was extremely happy both for Rose and Jean. Rose had family in Chicago, and Garth and Julia would see Rose and Jean regularly.

Jeanette Cartere and Sir Wooleyfin remained married and seemingly had a very happy life together. It turned out, however, that Wooley had an involuntary muscle spasm in his right eye, which led people to believe he was winking. Consequently, no one really has any insight into the intimate details of Jeanette's and Wooley's private life.

Former President Frank Karl refused a plea bargain, was tried and convicted of several counts involving art theft, fraud and conspiracy. He was sentenced to 132 years in a federal penitentiary in Nebraska. He served only three years when he was forked to death by twelve of his fellow inmates for stealing food off their plates. The event was known for years in the prison as "the great harpooning."

Agnes Schmidhausen never had another fainting spell. She lived several more years and continued to treat Julia as a granddaughter. She adored Garth and would regularly send him gifts, including a 1948 fully restored Jaguar XK120 Roadster. She insisted on driving it whenever she was in Chicago, wearing goggles and a flowing scarf. When she drove the car by herself, she would frequently get lost, and Garth would have to send out a search party to find her.

It should come as no surprise that Garth and Julia were married in a year. Agnes insisted on having the ceremony in her apartment. Before the wedding, Garth and Julia traveled to Paris where Garth asked Julia's father for her hand in marriage.

Julia spent almost every weekend with Garth after the award banquet, and then Julia was offered a visiting professorship at the acclaimed University of Chicago. Before the year was over, she was offered a permanent, tenured position. She sold her house in Manhattan and moved into the President's home in River Forest where Garth had taken up residency. She discontinued her work with the F.B.I., but not before bringing three other art thieves to justice.

Garth served two years as Interim President of Lortigue University. He performed superbly in the position. He was offered the permanent position, but declined it. He actually enjoyed the Presidency, but it demanded too much of his private time, time that he would rather spend with Julia. When he stepped down from the Interim Presidency, he returned to the Deanship of the College of Law, a position in which he took calculated and intelligent risks. He also arranged to purchase the house in River Forest because Julia felt it was home.

Garth would frequently watch Julia awaken in the morning, and he considered it among his most treasured privileges.

END NOTES

CHAPTER ONE

Lortigue University is a fictitious entity.

Neceau is a fictitious village.

The Schmidhausen Foundation is a fictitious entity.

The University of Chicago and Northwestern University are each highly regarded universities in Chicago, Illinois.

Macallan 18-Year-Old is a single malt Scotch, distilled and bottled by the Macallan Distillers, LTD, Easter Elchie's House at Craigellachie, Scotland.

CHAPTER TWO

Manor & Kling is a fictitious law firm.

RL is a restaurant in Chicago that is connected with the Ralph Lauren store on Michigan Avenue. Its entrance is on Chicago Avenue.

Glenrothes 1991 is a sweet single speyside malt Scotch distilled and bottled in Scotland by the Glenrothes Distillery, the corporate headquarters of which are located at 3 St. James Street, London.

Columbia University and Harvard University are each known to have excellent law schools.

CHAPTER THREE

The Iroquois Hotel is a small luxury hotel located at 49 West 44th Street in New York City. Except for inconsequential facts, it is accurately described in the story.

The "LSAT," or Law School Admissions Test, is accurately described in the story.

"Penn" refers to the University of Pennsylvania in Philadelphia, Pennsylvania. It was founded by Benjamin Franklin. Its business school, The Wharton School of Business, is among the best in the nation.

O'Hare is one of two major airports serving Chicago.

The New Yorker is a Conde Nast Publications magazine. It was founded in 1925 as a weekly magazine.

The Waldorf Astoria Hotel and the Waldorf Towers are accurately described in the story. The hotel is located at 301 Park Avenue. The Towers have hosted every U.S. President since Herbert Hoover. The apartments in the Towers range from 2,100 to 5,400 square feet.

CHAPTER FOUR

Le Cheval Blanc is a fictitious restaurant. At one time, there was a restaurant in New York City near 44th Street and 3rd Avenue known as Le Cheval Blanc. It is no longer there.

CHAPTER FIVE

Hunter College was founded in 1870 as a women's college. It is now a co-educational college that is part of the City University of New York. Its MA in Art History is one of the most comprehensive in the nation.

Christie's refers to Christie's Fine Art Auctioneer which has showrooms throughout the world, including New York City, Chicago, Geneva, London, Zurich and Paris.

"Degenerate art" is accurately described by Julia in the story. Lynn H. Nicholas, The Rape of Europa (1995).

"Old Master" is accurately described by Julia in the story. Oxford English Dictionary.

The "Hermitage Museum" in Saint Petersburg is accurately described by Julia in the story. Lynn H. Nicholas, The Rape of Europa (1995).

The Ralph Lauren Store on Madison Avenue in New York City is accurately described in the story.

Harvard College, Yale University, the Sorbonne and the Louvre are actual institutions.

"Degas," "Bellini," "Rembrandt," Signorelli," "Ruben," and "Renoir" are Old Master painters.

The name "Posse" is derived from a historical figure, "Hans Posse," who was authorized by Hitler to collect stolen art at Jeu de Paume in Paris for ultimate placement in the museum in Linz. Matthews' assistant's name, "Rose," is derived from Rose Valland who worked as a clerk at the Jeu de Paume under Posse. She was a spy for the Allied Forces and kept secret records of the art gathered at the Jeu de Paume. Lynn H. Nicholas, The Rape of Europa (1995).

Chamard's is a fictitious restaurant.

The Bordeaux is authentic.

Julia's description of Hitler's private library, and the subject of sorcery, is accurate. Kenneth D. Alford, Nazi Plunder (2000).

Louis Tannen Magic has been in existence since 1925. Prior to the internet, its catalogues were cloth bound books which are now collectors' items. The current store plays a role in a subsequent chapter of the story.

The "Matrix" and "The Ambitious Card" are magic tricks which are in many magicians repertoire. The Ambitious Card effect has been described as the trick that fooled Houdini. Alex Stone, Fooling Houdini (2012).

Julia's description of stolen artwork is factually based, albeit somewhat simplified as Julia acknowledges. Ulrich Boser, The Gardner Heist (2009); Kenneth D. Alford, Nazi Plunder (2000); Lynn H. Nicolas, The Rape of Europa (1995); The efforts of the United States to protect art in the immediate aftermath of World War II is factually based. Robert M. Edsel, The Monuments Men (2009).

CHAPTER SIX

Louis Tannen Magic is factually described in the story. It is open on Sundays, 10:00 to 4:00.

"Nickels to Dimes" is a popular trick for beginners.

"The Professor's Nightmare" is a standard trick sold in most magic stores.

The University of Chicago has a highly respected Art History department that was founded in 1902.

The "Peninsula" refers to the Peninsula Chicago, a hotel located at 108 East Superior Street. It is known for its "High Tea."

River Forest is accurately described in the story.

"Tiffany" refers to Tiffany & Co. which operates stores throughout the world.

CHAPTER SEVEN

The CADE and Plumpjack are authentic wineries in Napa, California.

CHAPTER EIGHT

The University Club is accurately described in the story. Franz Schulze, A Heritage: University Club of Chicago, 1887-1987 (1990).

The reference to Dominican University is factual. The college was originally founded in 1901 in Sinsinawa, Wisconsin and moved to its current location in River Forest in 1922.

Schoenling is a fictitious artist.

Hemmingway's Bistro is a restaurant near River Forest located in neighboring town of Oak Park.

CHAPTER NINE

Cabaret is a musical by Kander and Ebb which opened on Broadway in 1966. It won the Emmy for Best Musical in 1967. The song to which Karl refers is "The Money Song." The Money Song actually had two versions. In the original production, it was known as "Sitting Pretty." In the 1972 film, The Money Song was rewritten as "Money, Money," In the 1987 Broadway revival, both versions were incorporated into a single medley. Cabaret Songbook, 2nd Edition.

There are two Brooks Brothers clothing stores in Chicago. One is located at 209 South LaSalle Street. The other is located at 713 North Michigan Avenue.

The Italian Village is a popular Chicago restaurant located at 71 West Monroe Street. Established in 1927 it is reputed to be Chicago's oldest Italian Restaurant.

The reference in the story to the F.B.I's Art Theft Program is factually based, and the description of its operation in the story is accurate. http://www.fbi.gov/hq/cid/arttheft/arttheft.htm.

References to the United States Code are authentic.

CHAPTER TEN

New York Elegance, is a fictitious magazine.

The Hayden Planetarium operates as part of the American Museum of National History. It is located at Central Park West at 79th Street. The Hayden Planetarium has been in operation since 1935.

CHAPTER ELEVEN

Angland Brothers is a fictitious store.

Bistro Carvande is a fictitious restaurant.

The magic museums described are factual. Robert-Houdin is credited to be the father of modern magic, and Harry Houdini's stage name is derived from Robert-Houdin. Houdini's actual name was Erich Weiss. Ruth Brandon, The Life and Many Deaths of Harry Houdini (1993).

EPILOGUE

Each prison is fictitious.

Jaguar stopped production of automobiles for sale to the public between 1940 and 1946 because of World War II. In 1948, Jaguar introduced the XK120 Roadster at the Earl's Court Motor Show. The car was considered a major advancement over previous models in its performance and speed. The "120" refers to its top speed. It is an iconic vintage roadster. Heiner Stertkamp, Jaguar: The Complete Story (2008); Nigel Thorley, Jaguar, All The Cars (2003).

Made in the USA
Middletown, DE
17 August 2015